THE AMERICAN SOLDIER
COLLECTION 11:
MENDING HEARTS

Dixie Lynn Dwyer

LOVEXTREME FOREVER

Siren Publishing, Inc.
www.SirenPublishing.com

A SIREN PUBLISHING BOOK
IMPRINT: LoveXtreme Forever

THE AMERICAN SOLDIER COLLECTION 11: MENDING
HEARTS
Copyright © 2015 by Dixie Lynn Dwyer

ISBN: 978-1-63259-193-7

First Printing: May 2015

Cover design by Les Byerley
All art and logo copyright © 2015 by Siren Publishing, Inc.

Printed in the U.S.A.

PUBLISHER
Siren Publishing, Inc.
www.SirenPublishing.com

DEDICATION

Dear readers,

Thank you for purchasing this legal copy of Mending Hearts.

It is never easy to lose someone you love. So many times people wish for a second chance, or to just feel a hug from that person they loved so deeply, or even just to hear their voice or smell their cologne or perfume. To get a second chance is a miracle.

Alana gets that second chance and it takes her determined, stubborn, empathetic, daughter-of-a-Marine heart, to help make her man and his team love again and love for the first and last time.

Life is filled with miracles. Sometimes you have to fight really hard, and love a whole lot, to make those miracles happen.

May you enjoy the story.

Happy Reading.

Hugs!

~Dixie~

THE AMERICAN SOLDIER COLLECTION 11: MENDING HEARTS

DIXIE LYNN DWYER
Copyright © 2015

Prologue

Alana sat in the seat alongside Gabe's parents, Mike and Marcy. She was shaking with emotion but trying very hard to be strong. Strong like her own parents had taught her to be. Strong like the daughter of a Marine should be.

But this was worse than anything she'd ever experienced in her life. Twenty, and in love with Gabe Weathers, her first and only lover, and now he was gone. The man she'd given her virginity to. The one she told her secrets to, and the man she wanted to raise a family with.

It seemed like only yesterday he was knocking on her bedroom window late at night and confessing his need, his calling, to enlist into the Marine Corps. Alana supported him. She adored him and would move heaven and earth for the man. But now, looking at the empty seat where Gabe would always sit, was getting to be too much for her. The same yearly memorial and the feeling deep in her gut that made her believe Gabe was still alive. He wasn't MIA or a POW somewhere in the Middle East. No. He was alive, and she couldn't accept the fact that everyone else believed him to be dead. Including the government that had sent him in there.

She was losing herself more and more, year after year. She had to leave this town. She needed to leave this life and start anew. Otherwise, she might as well go MIA herself and maybe permanently.

She lowered her head and clasped her hands on her lap as she prayed to God while the preacher gave a blessing and spoke about the memories of the spirit and the happy times of the past. There were no more happy times to remember, just the empty seat, the lonely, sick sensation in her gut, and the reality that Gabe was never coming back. She'd lost him, just like she'd lost her father and her mother.

She was alone, and going solo seemed to work out best for her.

"Alana, would you like to say a few words before we close the ceremony?" Marcy, Gabe's mom, asked her. The woman was sweet and kind and suffered so deeply losing her oldest son.

Alana glanced at Gabe's cousin, Deanna. She was married to two men, Teddy and Jim, who were detectives in a town called Salvation. It was a good four hours from Scrantonville, but every year, Deanna would show up for the memorial ceremony. Three years. Three years and Alana was losing herself.

She nodded her head at Marcy as Deanna bit her lower lip and her eyes filled with emotion. Alana didn't like to speak about the past and Gabe anymore. Plus, it always seemed to upset Marcy. Gabe's mom knew how in love Alana and Gabe were, so Alana made it quick.

She stood up and turned toward the large group of family and friends. Most were familiar faces, but a few were new ones, maybe soldiers who'd retired from the service and now resided in Scrantonville. Others came in support of Gabe, a fellow Marine.

She cleared her throat and looked to Deanna for a little moral support. Deanna held her gaze steady. Something wasn't right. Teddy squeezed Deanna's hand.

Alana cleared her throat. She had to get through this. One last time and then she was leaving Scrantonville.

"I can't believe that it has been three years that we've all gathered here to remember Gabe. I see lots of familiar faces, and others as well. Gabe probably would reprimand us for doing this. He was always so humble."

She felt her eyes well up with tears as she looked around the room, her eyes landing on one gentleman. Older, definitely military by his stance, his stature, and focus as she spoke. She didn't know who he was, but she had seen him here before.

"I can remember the day when Gabe told me he wanted to enlist. He was excited, firm in his decision, and I supported him, knowing the risks but also knowing more so the pride, the calling he had. So instead of focusing on the loss of Gabe and so many others, I ask that you all continue to support our men and women in uniform everywhere. Those who have given the ultimate sacrifice and those who struggle with adapting back to civilian life. Gabe's parents and I have set up the organization Love Thy Soldier. Over the last three years, we have helped many of those military men and women returning from service to adapt to their new ways of living, to find employment, to aid in financial support, and we continue to do so. So please spread the word about our program and help to save our soldiers and let them know that we appreciate all they do. Thank you."

Alana walked back to her seat but not before catching the eye of that man in the back, the one with the military stance, the one who seemed to be watching her like a hawk.

The pastor ended the ceremony, and they all headed outside despite the chilly March temperatures.

"That was nice, Alana," Deana said as she hugged Alana.

"Thanks. It's so nice of you to come here. I know it's a bit of a way to travel in one day."

"Are you kidding me? We wouldn't miss it," Deanna said, and then Teddy and Jim gave her a hug hello. But Deanna looked away, and Alana felt as if she were hiding something from Alana. But what could it be? Maybe she just felt uncomfortable about coming out here every year. Alana knew that it was getting to her too, but Marcy and

Mike seemed to look at it as a way of healing and never forgetting Gabe.

"So how is work going? Any hope for that promotion?" Jim asked Alana.

"No hope. To be honest, I think it's time to look for something different," she told them as they stood by the sidewalk.

Other people were saying goodbye to Marcy and Mike, and she couldn't help but think about having to repeat this memorial next year at the same time. It was depressing, besides the fact that there was nothing to look forward to but this. All her friends she had had moved on, gotten married, or left in search of careers or lives outside of Scrantonville. Alana felt like a lost cause.

"What are you thinking about doing? I hear that Lance Masters is looking for a personal assistant in the law office in town," Jim told her.

She shook her head and then looked down toward the road that headed out of town and deeper into Texas Hill Country.

"Alana?" Deanna said her name, and then she felt her hand on her shoulder.

She didn't want to upset them, but it would be better to let them all know she was going to leave town. That she needed to breathe.

She felt the tears in her eyes. Leaving Scrantonville wasn't going to be so easy.

"I'm thinking about doing some traveling."

"Traveling? Like to where?" Deanna asked.

"Out of Scrantonville and deeper into Texas. Maybe even hop around a bit and check out places that Gabe and I talked about. I don't know." She felt that thick lump in her throat as she thought about Gabe.

"Honey, it's dangerous out there. You've never been out of Scrantonville. You can't just go off on your own," Deanna told her.

"I'll be fine," she told them.

"Deanna is right. You should reconsider. It's not like it seems in books and in movies. It's not so easy traveling on your own. You're an attractive young woman, and there are people who would take advantage of that," Jim told her.

"I can take care of myself. I've been doing it for quite some time, remember?" she said in a very firm tone. Both Jim and Teddy appeared uncomfortable, and Deanna looked upset again.

"Listen, I get it. Doing this yearly memorial and running the fundraising event can get overwhelming. But you don't need to leave the people who care about you and the place where you're safe."

"Don't tell me that, Deanna. You don't understand." Alana began to walk away and then turned back toward her.

"I can't breathe here. I can't do anything but think about Gabe. Everywhere I turn, everything I do, I see him or think of him."

"Aw, honey, that will change. With time, it will get easier."

She shook her head at Deanna.

"No. It's been three years. I'm going to be twenty-three soon, and what do I have to show for my life? There has to be something more. I can't imagine living alone forever and dying here. Hell, I'm dying right now, Deanna. I can't take it anymore. I can't live like this."

The tears began to flow, and Deanna pulled Alana into her arms and hugged her.

"I'm sorry, baby. I'm so sorry. I know it. I understand. Is this your final decision?" she asked, and Alana heard Deanna begin to say something else but change her mind.

"I'm suffocating. I have to leave."

Deanna nodded, and Jim and Teddy looked upset, but they supported her and offered any help she might need in the planning.

"I appreciate that, but I have to do this on my own."

"You call us if you need anything. Understand?" Teddy asked her.

She nodded and accepted their hugs before she watched them walk away. The decision was made. She was leaving Scrantonville and headed wherever her destiny led her.

Chapter 1

"I don't know what else we can do for him. He's non-responsive to anything the doctors and therapists have suggested," Jaxon Brothers told his three friends, Geno, Gator, and Jeb.

"It's so damn frustrating. To see him like this after the fight he put up to get through that cluster-fuck of a mess. Those damn terrorists fucked with his head," Gator added in his thick Southern accent. He was from New Orleans and was one big, bad-ass soldier, all six feet four inches of him, with muscles upon muscles, and that thick, hard voice that could cut through any crowd. Jaxon admired his friend, who was more like a brother, just as Geno, Jeb, and Gabe were.

Jaxon ran his fingers through his hair.

"Gabe's not coming out of this fog. It's like he wishes he were dead, yet something makes him hold on."

"Yeah, but then suggest going out and socializing and he turns into a beast. His sourness, nastiness, and aggression are too fucking scary to expose him to the public in Salvation. I don't think Garrett is right about pushing Gabe to start living again," Jeb told them.

"Garrett has had that limp of his for years, and he would know what it takes to get through the pain and the public scrutiny as people stared as he limped," Geno told them.

Jaxon looked at Geno, who was just as tall as him and in great physical condition. They all were. He wished there was some way to get through to Gabe and make him live his life again, instead of being such a prick.

"I don't think we're talking about the same thing here. Gabe is all fucked up. He's got that bad scarring, the indention where he lost the chunk of his muscle, and then the limp. He walks with a cane and has continuous pain," Jaxon stated.

"But if he doesn't get out and move around, try to do the exercises and things, then it will never improve. Sure, he may not walk without the limp, but he can get past the pain by working out those muscles. He just works out his upper body and his abs," Gator said.

"We're all trying to transition back to civilian life still, and it's been a year. We need to get him out more," Gator said.

"What are you thinking, Gator?" Jaxon asked him.

"A couple of weeks ago, we helped with that fundraiser for the school wrestling team with Wes. There's some other activities and volunteer work coming up. We could all participate together as a team. Gabe seems a lot better when we're all together. He would at least get out of the house and engage in some form of public activity. It might help him."

"It sure as shit can't hurt," Jaxon said.

"Well, I wouldn't say that." Jeb rubbed his chin. Just the other day as Jeb started in on Gabe and how he was being a depressed asshole, Gabe had decked him. It took Jaxon and Gator to separate the two before they pounded one another to death.

"Let's hope nothing like that happens again. I'm willing to give this a try. Something has to give," Jaxon told them, and they all agreed.

Jaxon couldn't help but think that this might be a mistake. He always worried about Gabe going off the deep end and losing his mind or becoming so violent that he would need to be restrained or could get arrested, or even placed in some psych ward. He wouldn't even let them tell his parents or family that he was alive and well. He was so mangled up when they'd found him in that building in Iraq that he just wanted to die. The more the doctors talked about his injuries and the lasting effects of the damage to his body, the more Gabe closed up and asked them to put him out of his misery. It was the worst time of all their lives, to see their best friend, their fellow soldier and brother, in pain and wanting to give up and die.

Something had to give. There had to be something that would make Gabe want to fight to live a better quality of life. Something.

* * * *

Alana looked at the small house she was renting. Well, it was more like a little cottage with everything on one floor. A large bedroom, no closet space, a big kitchen, and medium-sized living room space, but it also had a pretty back porch and a yard that led up to a woods. It was in a small town about thirty minutes from Salvation. She chuckled to herself. It seemed she didn't feel as confident as she'd thought she would feel being far from home. Instead, she'd chosen a place not too far from Deanna, Teddy, and Jim. They were thrilled, and Deanna even brought Julia over to the house with her. The three-year-old was adorable, and it made Alana think of Gabe. But then again, there wasn't much that didn't make Alana think of Gabe. Even though she'd left Scrantonville and headed away from the memories and the sadness, they had followed her here.

She looked around the room and knew she needed furniture. She needed something to focus on for today. It was Saturday, and Monday would come soon enough as well as working her two jobs. Monday, Wednesday, and Thursday, she worked from nine until two at the large clothing and household store in Tranquility, and on Friday and Saturday night, she worked as a waitress in Casper's. Thanks to Jim and Teddy. Their friends owned the place, and it was always very busy. Then on Sunday, her day off, she would clean the house and work on the handmade jewelry she created. She was trying to make enough items to sell at the large street fair in two weeks. She wasn't sure if she would sell anything, but Deanna offered her half the table she was setting up to sell her soaps and lotions from a known company.

Alana heard the horn honk and knew that Deanna was there to pick her up. She had called this morning and told Alana about an estate sale in a very old neighborhood in Salvation. Deanna told her she would be able to get some antique furniture at some good prices to place in her home and perhaps even some things for free. She grabbed her purse and her keys then locked the door before she headed down the cobblestone walkway. She really liked this small cottage. Despite the size, it had character and made her think of small towns and everything they had to offer. Tranquility was quiet and just beginning to get established.

"Good morning, sunshine. Are you ready to get all nostalgic?" Deanna asked, and Alana got into the front seat of the car.

"Nostalgic, huh? Well, I guess so. I've never been to an estate sale before."

"Oh, well then, this should be exciting for you. It's kind of weird going through a dead person's belongings, but the family is trying to raise money for the local sports teams. They're donating all the money."

"That's so nice. God, I hope I don't get the heebie-jeebies. I kind of have this sixth sense when it comes to spirits and things."

Deanna rolled her eyes.

"Oh brother. Please don't start talking to this dead woman aloud. Just keep the conversation to yourself."

Alana chuckled as they drove out of Tranquility.

"Who was the woman anyway?"

"Alana, isn't it better if you don't know anything about her?"

"No. I would like to know. We are going to be rummaging through her things, as you described."

Deanna laughed.

"Okay, well, from what I heard, she was very wealthy, and she was a collector of fine art. She also had a lot of costume jewelry from what the list of items available online said. She was a major part of the community many years back, and she was sort of a hoarder."

"A hoarder? Oh no, that's not good. Hoarders usually collect junk."

"Not this woman. Her junk was expensive, and supposedly, she was into mystical things." Deanna gave Alana a wink. Alana chuckled as they continued on their way to this estate in Salvation.

Thirty minutes later, they arrived, and there were only a few people coming and going.

"I don't know. It's a very old house but looks disheveled."

"Alana, she was very old and lived alone. It's not really disheveled anyway. It's kind of charming."

Alana shrugged and headed inside. The moment she entered the house, she felt a bit strange. There was a large winding staircase carpeted in a rich, burgundy color up the middle of each dark-wood-stained step. The wood on the railing was exquisite, and then Alana caught sight of all the things right there in the main entryway. There were racks of clothing that contained gorgeous evening gowns from a time well passed. If Alana had to guess, she would think they were from the twenties or thirties. There were gorgeous mirrors, a secretary's desk that had to be a hundred years old, and so much more.

"Hello, ladies. Is there something specific you were looking for today? I would be happy to help you," one older woman said as she greeted them hello. She looked so kind that Alana couldn't help but smile.

"I think we're just looking," she told her. The woman nodded but seemed a little sad.

"This is my first time walking through an estate sale. I'm not really sure what to do."

Her eyes lit up, and Deanna smiled at Alana.

"My name is Agnes."

"I'm Alana, and this is Deanna. This home is so beautiful and huge."

"I know it may seem overwhelming, but my Great-aunt Margaret was an amazing woman. She collected so many different things. Take your time and look around. If you see anything you like, just let me know, and we can talk cost."

"Oh, wonderful. Thank you," Alana said.

"I'm going to look over here at some of the kitchen things," Deanna told her.

"Okay, I'm just going to browse around," Alana said and then walked by the evening gowns and made her way through the front parlor and the back bedrooms.

It was odd, but Alana felt kind of funny walking through Margaret's home. The woman had only recently passed away, and it seemed strange to allow so many people to just walk through and see things, even buy them. But as she noticed people walking by and picking up items as though they were at a yard sale, she began to really look around. She climbed the back stairs that led to the second-floor bedrooms.

The second floor was even more stunning, and there were more closets with racks of clothing and people looking through them. There were brass and wood headboards, gorgeous pieces of furniture like large dressers and antique mirrors, an old-fashioned sewing machine, and even some ornaments and decorations. Then she noticed the displays of antique wooden boxes opened wide on a long, large dresser. There were beaded necklaces, mostly broken, and some in fairly good shape. Many of the patterns and colors caught her eyes, and she knew they would make the perfect additional pieces to jewelry she designed. She could reuse them and add them to certain pieces she had.

"Did you find something that you liked?" Deanna asked as she approached, carrying a pretty vase and some curtains.

"Yes, these beads. They would make some beautiful additions to my collection and materials I use to make my own jewelry. Look at this one. And this one." Alana showed them to Deanna.

"Those are very pretty and unique. It has a sticker of twenty dollars on it."

"Each?" Alana asked.

"No, silly, for the whole box. Look, this one says it too."

"Oh my, this is great. Do you think it's okay to take them all?"

"Of course. I bet Great-aunt Margaret would be happy to see you turn them into something amazing."

Alana chuckled and then turned to the right. That's when the piece of furniture under the large stacks of blankets caught her eye.

"Oh my, look at this, Deanna." Alana made her way closer and began to move the stacks of blankets to the side. She uncovered a desk that had multiple drawers in a golden wood color with etching and an antique finish. But this was authentic, not manufactured to look old and antiqued.

"God, that is a stunning piece. That could make a good work station for you."

"Yes, I was thinking the same thing. I love how unique it is and in such great condition." Alana opened the drawers to check them. Inside were strings and other materials, including small tools similar to what Alana used to make jewelry.

"Ah, so you found something. My aunt loved that desk. She used to make her own beaded necklaces and things. Some of her tools are still in there I think."

"That's what I like to do, too. I make my own jewelry."

"Oh, how wonderful. Do you sell them in the boutique in town?" Agnes asked Alana.

"Oh no, I haven't sold any yet. I was planning on trying to sell some at the fair coming up. Deanna is going to have a table with handmade soaps, lotions and other items."

Agnes ran the palm of her hand over the wood.

"This is a very special piece. I think it's meant to be yours, Alana."

"Really?"

"Definitely. You know, my great-aunt was a bit of a mystical woman who believed in the spirits and karma and all that stuff. She used to say that fate had a way of making things work out the way things were meant to be. Even if it took a long time, it eventually caught up. She had a lot of great sayings and beliefs in destiny."

"Well, I think your aunt would love for Alana to have this desk and to use it for her own beads and jewelry making. Alana was going to buy the two wooden chests of necklaces," Deanna told Agnes.

"The broken ones?" Agnes asked.

"They're so pretty and unique. I thought I could use them in some of the designs I create for the jewelry I make. I've never seen such pretty patterns and colors."

"Well, that's because a lot of them came from overseas. Some of these were beads of necklaces my aunt made herself." Agnes picked up one broken strand and watched the beads slide off and into the wooden box.

"I'm sure you can make something gorgeous from these."

"Well ,how much is the desk?" Alana asked.

"We priced it at $300.00 But you can have the desk, all those chests of beads, even the ones on the floor, and that Victorian-style floor lamp for $300. My great-aunt used to place that next to the desk so she could see all the tiny beads and string she used."

"Wow, that would be wonderful. I'll take them."

"We have to leave the desk and come back later tonight for it though. It won't fit in my car," Deanna told Agnes.

"That's okay. We have some men who volunteer to deliver purchases in the area."

"I live in Tranquility," Alana told her.

"Oh, well, a couple of the men here today live there. They can probably drop it off to you on their way home."

"Wonderful. Here's the money for everything."

Alana pulled out her wallet and took out the $300 she had.

"We can deliver the beads the lamp and everything. Why don't you continue to look around, and I'll make sold signs up for these."

"Agnes, do you need anything delivered now?"

She heard the deep voice, and both Alana and Deanna turned around to see a very tall, muscular man standing in the doorway.

"Actually, Alana here just purchased the desk, the lamp, and all these chests of beads. She lives your way in Tranquility. Maybe on your way home, you and the men could drop these off to her?"

"Sure thing, miss. Just write down your address, and we'll drop it off and carry it inside for you."

"That would be great," Deanna replied, but Alana couldn't seem to find her voice.

The man was quite attractive and big. He had dark brown wavy hair, big blue eyes, and a tattoo on his bicep that showed slightly from beneath the T-shirt he wore. He held her gaze and gave her a kind smile as Deanna gave her arm a nudge.

"You said you wanted to look around a little more. Come on. Let's make sure that there's nothing else this kind man needs to deliver later to your house," Deanna teased.

"The name's Jeb, miss."

"Nice to meet you, Jeb. I'm Deanna, and this is Alana. It's her house you'll be delivering the furniture to."

"Great. Nice to meet you. Both," he added, although he held only Alana's gaze, not Deanna's.

Agnes chuckled.

"Well, meet us downstairs when you're done. I'm getting a sold sign for these things, Jeb," Agnes told him, and Deanna and Alana began walking.

"Nice guy. Big," Deanna added as they continued to look around.

* * * *

Jeb couldn't seem to take his eyes off of the pretty, petite brunette he'd just met. She had gorgeous green eyes, full lips, and a body that instantly made his body react. That was different. He never got all hard just from checking out some woman. She seemed young, and yet mature, maybe even sophisticated. Either way, as he walked downstairs to grab Gator, he was still thinking about the woman.

"Hey, we got a delivery to make at the end of the day," he told Gator, who was rolling up some rope they'd just used on another delivery right in Salvation.

"No problem. Is it something big?" Gator asked.

Jeb was looking up toward the stairs as Alana and her friend were walking down. Gator gave Jeb's back a tap.

"Is it me, or is that an angel descending the stairs?"

Jeb half chuckled at Gator's description. Through the stained glass, the sunlight shot rays of colored lights over the staircase and against the lower walls. As Alana walked down them, she sure did look like an angel. A pretty little delicate one. His heart hammered in his chest.

"Are you still browsing?" Jeb asked her.

"I don't think so. I didn't come here with that much money or expecting to buy a lot," Alana told him.

"Well, that piece you picked upstairs is gorgeous." He licked his lower lip as he looked her body over. She was pretty damn gorgeous too. Her friend, who appeared a little older, chuckled as she walked by.

Gator cleared his throat. Alana looked away from Jeb and to Gator. She looked intimidated as she quickly lowered her eyes and took a step back. Gator was a pretty big man. Big muscles and wide shoulders, plus tall. He towered over most men.

"This is my friend, Gator. Gator, meet Alana. We'll be delivering some furniture and things to her on our way home later."

Gator reached his hand out for her to shake. She didn't hesitate as she smiled softly at him.

"Nice to meet you, miss."

Jeb watched the exchange. He saw the instant attraction and something happen when Alana and Gator's hands touched. They both paused and then quickly pulled back. Gator's eyes roamed over Alana's body. She looked away shyly, then back again. Excitement began to bubble in his gut.

She pulled back.

"Oh, here's my address. Do you know where it is?" she asked Jeb as she handed him the slip of paper. When their fingers touched, her lower lip dropped, and she quickly pulled back.

"Sure, darling, this isn't far from our place at all." He handed the slip of paper to Gator as he kept his eyes glued to Alana's green eyes. She was breathtaking. She had to have a boyfriend. Shit, that pissed him off. He was shocked as he wondered why he was so instantly attracted to the young woman and why the thought of her with a boyfriend angered him.

"I know this place. It's a pretty little cottage behind Ron Jackson's place. God, they used to have this big garden in the back. It was something else," Gator told her.

Her eyes widened, and she seemed encouraged to continue talking.

"What else do you know about the cottage?"

"It belonged to Ron's aunt. She was a really nice lady, and one of the first main residents of Tranquility. You know it's a fairly new town? But growing in leaps and bounds," Gator told her.

"I noticed that there aren't a lot of storefronts. Not like Salvation," Alana replied.

"I think the town wants to keep it very low-key. There's not much for sale, and a lot of the land is owned privately. I don't think there's much available to buy or build on. Though it seems when someone needs a place, something pops up," Jeb added.

Jeb watched her step out of the way as a few people walked past, trying to head to the stairs.

"Yes, it's funny you say that. When I came into Tranquility looking for a place to rent, there didn't seem like anything was available. No signs, no vacancies. I asked around and stopped into the small café there, and after talking to one of the waitresses, I found out that the cottage was available to rent."

Jeb smiled. He knew how things operated in Tranquility. It was like some secret society of helpers. As people came into town looking for a new place to settle down, or perhaps passing through or looking for trouble, the town's people would evaluate them, and if they saw them in need and that the person was good and kind, they worked out making something available for them to live in. It was interesting and definitely helped him and the rest of their team when they retired from the military. He had hoped the new town, and unknown faces, would make Gabe feel more secure. No such luck.

"Alana, Agnes said there are some things outside too, like porch swings and outdoor furniture. Weren't you looking for a rocking chair or something for the back porch while you're reading?" Deanna interrupted.

"Oh yes. I guess we can take a look."

"We're headed out there. We can show you around," Gator suggested, and Jeb felt that excitement in his gut again. It seemed Gator found Alana to be just as interesting and attractive as Jeb did.

* * * *

Alana felt something in the pit of her stomach as she walked outside along with Deanna, Jeb, and Gator. Both men were very big, attractive men, with muscles and tattoos on their arms, and both were very charming. It made her feel uneasy, almost sick to her stomach. That was how she often got when men flirted with her. It was almost like a guilty feeling, and felt as if she were cheating on Gabe. It was silly. Gabe was gone, and she needed to move on. But that was easier said than done.

"Hey, we can take a little lunch break now," some other man called over to them.

Alana looked, her eyes landing on another attractive man, an older-looking one with blond hair wearing a pair of blue jeans, a dark green T-shirt, and cowboy boots.

"Okay, Jaxon," Jeb called out as another guy looked at her when he came around from the truck.

She couldn't believe how attractive these men were as she absorbed their good looks and took in how tall and muscular they were. She felt so petite. She was lost in thought when she heard the gasp.

Swinging her head around toward Deana, she saw her friend's eyes well up with tears. Alana had swung back around to see what had upset her when she saw him.

There, by the front of the truck, stood a man who resembled Gabe. Her Gabe.

He paused, leaning on the cane he held by his side, and anger filled his sunken eyes.

"Gabe?"

Deanna called out his name, and Alana couldn't move. She was trying to process what was happening here as she felt the tears roll down her cheeks and the silence consume the air around her.

Deana stopped short as the man who resembled Gabe turned away.

"Gabe?"

Deanna said his name again, and the other two men who were by the truck went to her side. Alana was crying as she walked, ran toward the man she knew now was definitely Gabe, but who also seemed to be hiding from them. He limped around to the other side of the truck. Jeb and Gator followed her, as did Jaxon and the other guy too.

"Gabe, wait," Alana called out, and she reached for his arm. The feel of muscle and the connection they shared, still as strong and fierce as ever, electrified her entire body.

"Go away. I don't want to see you," he snapped at her.

Fury, anger, and hatred… Emotions like she had never seen in Gabe's eyes before greeted her tears and the power of her emotions.

"Gabe why? I thought you were dead. Everyone thinks that you're dead," she told him.

Strong hands gripped her shoulder from behind.

She didn't look back. She used that strength to speak, to process and get out her thoughts.

"Gabe, you're alive," she whispered, and Deanna was by her side crying, reaching for Alana's hand.

"I'm not alive. I'm dead. Go away, Alana. Just leave me alone." He limped away.

"No. Why are you doing this, Gabe?" she cried, and the person holding her shoulders turned her around. She locked gazes with Jaxon. His bold blue eyes bore into hers.

"How do you know Gabe? Who are you?" He questioned her as if he were interrogating her.

"I thought he was dead," she whispered.

"Where does he live? How long has he been here in Salvation? Is he okay? What happened to him? Why is he hiding from his family?" Deanna rambled on.

Gator rubbed his chin and looked fierce and sad at the same time.

Jaxon ran a hand along Alana's hair and then cupped her cheek.

"How do you know Gabe? Are you family?"

She shook her head.

"He was my boyfriend. We were going to get married." She then began to sob.

Jaxon pulled her into his arms and hugged her tight. She didn't care that she didn't know him or these other men. She knew they knew Gabe and were friends of his, perhaps men he trusted to be around.

"Put that phone away. Don't call anyone," Jeb ordered, and Alana looked to the side and saw Deanna with her cell phone in her shaking hand.

"His parents need to know that he's alive and well. We've all been sick and thought he was dead," Deanna told them.

"He doesn't want anyone to know that he's alive," Jaxon told them as they heard the truck pull away with Gabe and the other man whose name Alana didn't know.

Alana's heart was pounding inside of her chest. She could hardly catch her breath as the situation played out over and over again in her head.

Gabe isn't dead. He's alive, and he wants nothing to do with me. Nothing.

* * * *

Jaxon walked Alana toward the set of outdoor chairs so she could sit down. So many thoughts were going through his head. Gabe had never mentioned Alana. He never once brought up a woman from his past that he had been in love with and was going to marry.

"Oh God, Alana, this can't be real," Deanna stated.

Jeb was standing there, and Gator squeezed Alana's shoulder.

"He looked so angry and his eyes… His eyes were dark, dull and hollow. Why wouldn't he want to see me? Why would he pretend to be dead?" she asked and sniffled.

Jeb knelt down and placed his hand on Alana's knee. The sight stirred something inside of Jaxon. They had all been checking Alana out when she came outside, but then the two women recognized Gabe.

"Gabe's been through a lot. It took all of us to get him to come out here today to volunteer to help. He usually doesn't go anywhere," Jeb whispered.

Alana's shoulders shook as she sniffled and then wiped the tears from her eyes with the back of her sleeve.

"We just had our yearly memorial for him in town. It's been three years," she said.

Jaxon was shocked as Jeb reached up and wiped away the tears.

"I couldn't even imagine how hard this has been for you. For both of you," Jeb said, looking at the other woman.

"I'm Gabe's cousin, Deanna. My mom is his mom's sister. My God, Aunt Marcy and Uncle Mike are going to freak out when they find out that Gabe is alive. I have to call my husbands. They were close to Gabe too."

"I don't think that's such a good idea," Jaxon said.

"Definitely not a good idea," Gator added.

"Why not? There are people who love him. Lots of people come to the memorial every year, and there's even a fundraiser we do for soldiers returning from serving, in honor of Gabe," Alana said as another tear rolled down her cheek.

Jaxon thought she was gorgeous. He felt the tug on his heart as he wondered why Gabe would not want to come back to her.

"You said your husbands? Do they live around here?" Jeb asked Deanna.

"No, we live farther out, in Salvation. To think that Gabe has been less then ten minutes away this whole time is outrageous," Deana told them.

"It is, but like we said, he doesn't go out at all," Gator told her.

"What's wrong with his leg? Why is he hiding?" Alana asked.

"He was badly injured during a mission. He was held prisoner in some shithole for months. Some of the men he was with never made it out, and the others died soon after they were rescued," Jaxon explained.

"He's dealing with a lot of emotions, Alana. We've tried lots of things to get through to him. Staying together as a team has helped him. Hell, it's helped all of us," Jeb added.

"You were part of the same team?" Alana asked.

She held Jaxon's gaze, and Jaxon felt that tightness again and an instant attraction. She was really sweet, almost angelic.

"Yes, ma'am. We served in a special unit together and hit it off immediately. Seems none of us want to part," Jeb told her, holding her gaze.

Alana looked away.

"Listen, he's going through a really hard time. It could last a while," Jaxon told her.

She looked back toward him and stood up, Jeb's hand falling from her leg. The tears rolled down her cheeks as she shook her head.

"Let's go, Deanna. Please," she said.

Jeb stood up, and he placed his hands into his pockets. He looked at Jaxon, who could see the concern on Jeb's face.

"It might be better to not let anyone else know that you saw Gabe today," Gator called out to Alana and Deanna.

"We'll see," Deanna said, placing her arm over Alana's shoulder.

They all watched them walk away, tears flowing, sadness overwhelming the two women, and there was nothing they could do.

"That was intense," Jeb whispered as he ran his fingers through his hair, and then he exhaled.

"I can't believe that Gabe never told us about her," Gator added.

"The war fucked him up. He's angry and combative all the time and with everyone," Jeb replied.

"I feel badly for Alana. That look on her face when she saw Gabe… My God," Gator added.

"I know. Hopefully Geno was able to get Gabe to talk about it and to calm him down. I was worried he might actually lash out at the two women," Jaxon told them as he walked toward the truck to grab more rope.

"Gabe would never hurt a woman. Didn't you see that look in Gabe's eyes when he locked onto Alana? They brightened up for half a second, and then he put up that wall of his," Gator said.

Jaxon had seen it. He'd also felt the sting of envy, knowing that Gabe had a woman like Alana as his girlfriend and knowing how screwed up Jaxon was himself that he could never have a committed relationship with anyone. Too many skeletons in the closet.

"It's going to be awkward delivering that furniture to Alana's place," Gator told them.

"I don't know. I wouldn't mind seeing her again. I felt badly for her and Deanna, Gabe's cousin. What a hell of a way to find out the guy you thought was dead was actually alive and well," Jeb stated.

"Yeah, what a hell of a way to find out. Let's get the next few deliveries done and then take that last one to Alana's place," Jaxon told Jeb and Gator.

"Should you call Geno to check on Gabe?" Jeb asked.

"I'm not quite ready to talk with him yet," Jaxon said and then walked back toward the house to see what delivery was next. He wanted to get through them and make this day end. Yet he also wanted to see Alana again, and he told himself it was because he felt badly for her. He swallowed hard but felt that sixth sense kick in. The one that told him this situation wasn't over with Alana. Not by a long shot.

* * * *

"Are you going to be okay?" Deanna asked Alana as she stood by her back porch looking out at the woods.

"You and I talked about this for the last two hours. What choice do we have? You saw him, Deanna. He wanted nothing to do with me, with us."

"Maybe he's suffering from one of those post-traumatic stress disorders or something? Or maybe something happened while he was serving. You know, Jaxon said he was held prisoner."

"Whatever it was, whatever happened to him, he's not the same man I knew. The man I love," Alana said and then covered her mouth to try and hide the sob.

Deanna pulled her close and hugged her as tears rolled down her cheeks.

"I don't think I'll be able to keep this from Teddy and Jim. I've never lied to them or withheld information."

"I know. Do what you feel is right."

Deanna looked out toward the wooded area and then to the old shed by the neighbor's house next door.

"It's kind of creepy out here. You sure this place is okay for you?"

"Deanna, don't worry. I've got my guns."

Deanna smiled.

"That's right. The daughter of a Marine."

"Yup." Alana walked Deanna out of the house. She waved goodbye and then headed back inside.

Now that she was alone, she pulled out a picture of Gabe. The real Gabe. The one who'd said he would love her forever. She traced the wooden frame with her finger and smiled at his masculinity and happy expression. Today, he hadn't looked happy. He looked withdrawn, sick, pale, and angry. For a split second, when he spotted her, she thought she saw excitement, love in his eyes, but just as quickly, it disappeared, and he told her he was dead.

He wasn't the man she knew. The one who spoke so sweetly to her, with passion and love. So many times over the last three years she'd gone over those great times she had with Gabe. They made her laugh. They made her cry, but there was also that sensation of feeling as though he was still alive. Now she knew it was more than a sensation. They were bound to one another.

She gulped, trying to swallow the lump of emotion down her tight throat. Her nose tingled, and her nostrils flared as she grabbed the pillow and cried.

* * * *

Gator and Jeb showed up at Alana's house to drop off the furniture and the items she had purchased. As Jeb walked up the front walkway, he could see down the side of the house and noticed someone standing by a tree. At first he thought it might be Alana, but then the person moved, and through the branches, Jeb could tell it was a man. He turned around as if he'd noticed Jeb had noticed him and then walked farther into the woods. Jeb got a very eerie feeling inside.

"What's wrong?" Gator asked him as he carried two of the boxes.

He explained about the guy, and now Gator was concerned.

"I hope it wasn't some Peeping Tom."

"Me too. We should inform Alana and make sure she's safe."

He rang the doorbell, and it took her some time to get there. When she opened the door, Jeb could tell that Alana had been crying. Her eyes brightened at the sight of them as she probably remembered the things she'd bought at the estate sale.

"I'm sorry. I totally forgot about the stuff being delivered. Can you give me a minute to move some boxes?" she asked.

"Sure thing, doll. Take your time," Jeb told her.

He watched her push some boxes around, and he couldn't help but to check out her butt as she bent over. Gator cleared his throat, and Alana looked up as she stood.

"This should be enough room. The place is small, so I need to use the living room as my office too."

"You picked a really nice piece. It has lots of drawers but isn't too big. It will be great right there," Jeb told her as he absorbed the pleasant scent of her home combined with her perfume.

"Where would you like me to put these?" Gator asked, holding two boxes of beads she had purchased.

"Oh, right down there on the rug is fine. I'll need to get organized," she whispered then had a far off look as she crossed her arms and appeared sad again.

"We'll get the piece," Jeb told her.

"She looks so sad. Been crying," Gator whispered.

"I know," was all Jeb could say. He felt badly too.

They got the piece down off the back of the truck, placed the lamp that came with it on top, too, and began heading up the sidewalk. Gator glanced toward the woods. "Did you mention the guy in the woods yet?"

Jeb shook his head. Alana held the door open.

They placed it down on the rug where she had cleared a spot, and Jeb and Gator complimented the location as Jeb fixed the lamp.

"This is perfect, and it doesn't take up too much room," Jeb said as he glanced around the small cottage.

"Listen," Jeb continued. "I'm not sure if you lock your doors or sit out back at night, but when we pulled up, I saw some guy in the woods. He was just standing there, and it looked like he was looking this way. Not positive, but wanted to be sure you were aware of it. You never know who might be lurking around in that woods. It's pretty big."

Her eyes widened, but she didn't freak out like he expected. She calmly replied.

"Thank you for telling me. I'm sure it was nothing, but you're right. You never can tell. I do lock the doors. I've lived alone for quite some time."

Her eyes filled up with tears, and she covered her mouth with her hand.

"Aw, honey. Don't cry," Jeb said and placed his hands on her shoulders. A moment later, he pulled her into his arms.

The feel of her against his body aroused him but also gave him this overwhelming need to protect her and make her happy. It just wasn't fair that such a pretty young thing was hurting. It made him feel pissed off at Gabe, yet the soldier in him understood.

"It's going to be okay," Gator whispered and caressed her hair.

Suddenly she lifted her head up.

"Oh God. I'm so sorry. I didn't mean to make you both feel uncomfortable. Can I get you a drink?"

"I don't think—" Gator began to say.

"Sure," Jeb interrupted and placed his hands in his pockets.

The scent of Alana's perfume and shampoo lingered in the air around him. He wondered if his shirt would smell like her even later as they drove back to the ranch.

She walked toward the kitchen and opened the door to the refrigerator. After pulling out two waters, she came back and handed them out.

"Thank you," Jeb said, holding her gaze. Gator said thank you, too, and then stared at her.

"You moved in pretty recently, huh?" Gator asked, breaking the silence.

"Yes, only about three weeks ago. It's a lot to get used to. But with working two jobs, I haven't had a lot of time to unpack everything," she told them.

"Two jobs?" Gator asked as Jeb was thinking the same thing. Why was this woman having to work two jobs? She lived alone. Or so it seemed. Maybe she had debt. Lots of women over shopped or had bad spending habits. Although Alana didn't seem the type at all.

She shrugged.

"Just keeping busy. Trying to just live, I guess," she said in a sad voice.

"Where are you working?" Gator thought to ask.

"Well on Mondays, Wednesdays, and Thursdays, I work at the clothing store in Salvation, and on Fridays and Saturdays, I work at Casper's waitressing and doing some bartending."

"Really? We go into Casper's often. I think I would remember seeing you," Gator told her, looking her over.

Alana pulled her bottom lip between her teeth. "Well, I just got started there last weekend. Deanna's husbands' friends own the place. They hooked me up with the job."

"You mean the McCallisters?" Jeb asked.

"Yes. You know them?"

"Of course we do. Gunner is a Texas Ranger, and Jaxon and Geno do some work for the local law enforcement. They train the cadets in the academy," Jeb said.

"That's great."

They all fell silent, and Jeb couldn't help but absorb Alana's beauty and watch her. She really was sweet. If only this situation with Gabe were different.

"Can I ask you two something?" Alana looked at both of them and then moved farther into the living room.

"Sure," Gator replied.

"How long have you guys and Gabe lived in Salvation?"

Jeb's heart sank a little. He almost felt jealous that she wanted to know about Gabe, yet he understood how difficult of a situation this was. He needed to put aside his attraction to her and just do the right thing.

"We've been here for a little over two years. We have a large ranch about ten minutes from here," he told her.

"Ten minutes?" She pulled her bottom lip between her teeth. Her voice cracked.

"I don't want to put the two of you in an awkward situation. It's just that you live with Gabe, a man I thought died while serving our country. To show up here, of all places, and bump into him, alive and fairly well at an estate sale is…well… pretty freaking crazy."

Jeb and Gator nodded.

"I'm certain it's been difficult," Jeb told her.

"To see an old boyfriend like that is freaky," Gator added.

"He was more than that. He left with the intention of us getting married and starting our lives together when he returned. He told me to wait for him, and I did."

Jeb swallowed hard.

"Surely you moved on after he was reported as MIA?" he asked.

She shook her head. "Move on? No. I didn't."

"Not even one guy since he left?" Gator questioned, as if she were lying.

She immediately got on the defensive. "No, not one guy. I declined any offers. I truly thought he would return to me."

They were all quiet a few seconds.

"Well, things change, Alana. You heard what he said. He doesn't want anyone to know he's alive. He's changed," Jeb told her.

"I've changed too, but I still care about him. I want to know what's wrong with him. What happened to him, and why is he shutting me out?"

"Those are questions we can't answer. It might be best to move on," he told her, feeling his gut clench. He had a loyalty to Gabe, but he was also a man.

"That's easier said than done, Jeb." She walked toward the door and opened it, a sure sign she was sending them on their way.

"Thank you for delivering the furniture."

"You're welcome. Good luck with it and with your new place," Gator said as he walked out first.

"Maybe I'll see you at Casper's or in town," Jeb said, and he didn't know why. He should just let it be.

"Maybe. Bye," she said, and he winked before he exited the house with her, closing the door behind them.

"God damn, she's beautiful," Gator whispered through clenched teeth as Jeb started the truck and headed out of her driveway.

He was grateful to hear that Gator was just as affected by Alana as he was.

"This situation is fucked up. I like her, too."

"Hell, that's obvious, and what's not to like? She's gorgeous, petite, sweet, and damn vulnerable right now."

"Some dick could come along and take advantage of that vulnerability. Especially with her working at Casper's," Gator told him.

"I know. She needs protection."

"Is that what we're calling it? The fact that we're attracted to her, and so is Jaxon, and we don't want some guys hurting her?" Gator asked.

"It is what it is."

Gator chuckled.

"This isn't a smart idea. You know that, right?"

"I don't know anything anymore. I just know I'm tired of feeling empty inside. I'm sick of seeing Gabe looking ready to take his own life. Jaxon said that Gabe's eyes lit up when he first saw Alana. There was something there."

"But it isn't there now. Gabe is all fucked up."

"I think we should watch over her."

"I think you want to do more than that to her."

Jeb gripped the wheel. She did feel good in his arms, all petite and him towering over her, encasing her body. He could just imagine what she would feel like naked against his skin with his dick buried deep in her pussy. But it wasn't right to have these feelings. She was Gabe's. Maybe he was attracted to her because the guys were all so close. Hell, he'd give his life for any of them, and they would do the same for him. He knew that. The connection was strong, deeper than blood. But still, Alana was young, an old flame of Gabe's. She obviously still cared for him. She kept shedding tears. He was being a dick.

"Don't feel like a dick. I felt it, too. Made me reconsider the whole ménage thing we once discussed," Gator confessed, and Jeb shot a look at him, nearly going off the road from Gator's statement. Gator was the least into commitments.

"We've fucked the same woman before, Gator. What are you talking about?"

"Pursuing this instant attraction to Alana. With Alana, it would be different. I know it would be. Besides, the others we screwed were meaningless. We were needy, so were they, and it worked out the few times we did it. I didn't feel an inkling of the…interest I feel around Alana, and we just met her. How the fuck is that even possible?"

Jeb shook his head. "You're fucking older than me. How the hell am I supposed to know?"

Gator grunted. "We're so fucked, you know that?"

"Yeah, I know. But like I said, it is what it is. We'll deal with it."

* * * *

Alana considered calling Marcy and Mike, Gabe's parents, numerous times. But then Deanna talked her out of it, and they were her blood relatives, not Alana's. She had three restless nights, and work seemed to go by too quickly. She was actually excited that Casper's was so crowded on Friday night. But then one waitress called in sick, and they were short a bartender. The McCallisters were furious. But then Gia, Gunny, Garrett, and Wes's wife showed up to help waitress, along with another friend, so Alana was asked to bartend.

She was a little rusty at first, but it was so crowded that she got the hang of things very quickly.

"Darling, you get that sexy little ass on over here and get me and my buddies another round. There's no need to help any other customers but us tonight," one cowboy called to her. He was feeling pretty good already and appeared to be swaying on the stool. His buddies chuckled, but the one guy kept those dark eyes glued to Alana, giving her the creeps.

Before she could say a word, Gator appeared. He slapped the guy on the shoulder way harder than a friendly hello between men would warrant.

"I think you're cut off, Sawyer. That's no way to speak to a beautiful lady," Gator said, and the guy shot him a look.

Gator squeezed in, knocking Sawyer nearly off the stool. Jeb and another guy joined him. Gator gave her a wink and a smile and then licked his lower lip as he took in the sight of her.

"Bartending now, huh? Be careful, they might make you a manager," he teased.

"Hi, Gator. Hello, Jeb."

"This is Geno. You didn't really get a chance to meet him last week." Gator introduced them, and Geno stuck out his hand as he leaned closer to the bar.

She locked gazes with his deep mocha-colored eyes and felt her heart begin to race. Seemed these men around here were mighty fine indeed.

"Nice to meet you. What can I get you guys?" she asked.

"We're still waiting on our beers, sugar," Sawyer said, interrupting them. "Why don't you make those first then come on over here and deliver them to me? If ya sit on my lap, maybe you'll get a nice tip."

Sawyer's buddies laughed, but Gator got pissed off. He grabbed the guy by his collar and pulled him up off the stool.

"You owe her an apology."

"For what? She's the bartender. She's going to serve me." He smirked then ran a hand along his crotch. Again his buddies laughed, but Gator, Jeb, and Geno got angry.

She was shocked when Gator lifted the guy by his collar and threatened him.

"It's time for you and your crew of shit to leave. This is a respectable place. She deserves respect and not your vulgar attitude."

"Fuck you, Gator," Sawyer said, and then he pulled back and went to swing.

Alana gasped. "Gator, it's okay."

"Take him out, Gator," someone called out.

"Knock him on his ass," another guy yelled.

In a flash, Gator, Jeb, and Geno, along with the McCallisters, were tossing Sawyer and his buddies out of the bar.

"Are you okay, Alana?" John Luke, one of Garrett's dads, asked her as he placed his hand on her shoulder.

She was shaking a little, worried that the guys were going to get into some kind of trouble over helping her. That guy Sawyer was just drunk. She wasn't worried about him. She was worried about Gator, Geno, and Jeb.

"I'm fine. I'm so sorry that happened."

"Sorry? It wasn't your fault. Sometimes these guys get a little rowdy, and sometimes they even get hauled off by the police. They're just letting off some steam. But it seems you've got your own security team there. Good men. They're heroes, those three. Their whole team is," John told her, and she wondered what he meant, but before she could ask, Gator, Geno, and Jeb returned.

Men were shaking their hands and smiling and joking with them as they complimented their work, and Alana poured three beers from the tap and placed them down on the counter. She felt a bit strange right now. She didn't need people thinking she was involved with these men in a romantic way. That sudden thought did something to her as she quickly breathed through the instant tightness in her chest and that feeling of anxiety.

"It's all good, right, darling?" Geno asked her and gave her a wink.

"You guys didn't need to do that. I'm sure Sawyer and his buddies were harmless," she said, and they reached for the beers.

"I think we're better judges of that, Alana," Gator said in a very hard tone.

"What's that supposed to mean? I can take care of myself. I don't need some jarheads to protect me," she snapped, and he raised one eyebrow at her as Jeb and Geno just stared at her and smirked.

She wiped down the counter and looked away until she felt the large hand over her wrist and hand, and Gator's eyes locked onto hers.

"Darling, no need to get pissed. They were being assholes. Any of us would love the opportunity to teach them a lesson."

"Well, I could have handled that. It's all I'm saying," she told him, and he released her wrist and hand and gently glided a finger along her jaw.

"He was out of line and three times your size. At least he'll reconsider being disrespectful to you the next time," Gator told her and then leaned back onto the stool.

"If there is a next time, I get to throw him out on his ass," Geno said and chuckled, and then Jeb did too, lightening up the confrontation she had with Gator.

He sure was a big man. He displayed intimidation well.

* * * *

Gator was furious. He couldn't believe how pissed off he got hearing Sawyer talk to Alana like that. She was a classy young woman who deserved respect. Even in the black V-neck T-shirt with the Casper's logo on it and her tight blue jeans, she looked amazing. As she turned away and went toward another group of guys to take their drink orders, he watched her ass and the way she filled out those blue jeans. He caught the eyes of the other men roaming over her abundant breasts and then to her gorgeous face. It fueled his anger, and he realized he was fucking jealous.

He took a deep breath and cursed as he turned away. He couldn't look. He couldn't watch more men undress her with their eyes and hear their flirty comments.

"This is going to be a long fucking night," Jeb stated with his arms crossed in front of his chest.

Geno took a sip from his beer and kept his eyes on Alana. His expression was calm. How the fuck could he be so calm?

"Just relax. We're here and keeping an eye on things. Men are going to flirt with her. Look at her. She's fucking hot, and she smells incredible," Geno whispered, his eyes never leaving Alana's body.

"Are Jaxon and Gabe coming here too? Maybe it's not such a good idea," Jeb told Gator.

"Hell if I know. Gabe was in a shit-ass mood. Jaxon talked with him, or at least tried to, and got nowhere. Gabe won't discuss his relationship with Alana and why he doesn't even want to talk with her," Gator told Jeb.

"It's all part of his recovery process. The life, the things he did and had before the war don't exist. They were another time, another place, when he was a different man," Geno told them, and Gator turned around to face him.

"What?"

"Don't look at me like you don't get it. We've all been where Gabe is. Maybe not to the extent because the rest of us haven't sustained any permanent physical injuries, just psychological. Gabe's got a chuck of flesh out of his leg, remnants of the shrapnel imbedded in his body, and he can't walk without the cane. Any of you think that maybe he feels less of a man?"

Gator ran his hand over his mouth.

"Fuck, no. Gabe's always been such a gung ho hard-ass fuck. He never gave up, always had the drive, the determination to overcome obstacles and not be defeated. Hell, he was top of our training group on Special Teams. I watched him complete some of those crazy obstacle courses. Hell, I watched him locate and destroy potential terrorist operatives before they could strike and kill unknowing US soldiers. The man was meant to be a soldier, a Marine."

"Exactly," Geno said then glanced back down toward the end of the bar.

"Look who's talking to Alana now," Jeb interrupted as he slid off his seat and moved closer to the bar.

Gator turned to look and nearly bit the inside of his cheek.

"Haslow Walker and his three buddies. Special Forces and so damn arrogant since they claimed the title of best team marksmen in the fall shooting competition," Gator whispered.

"We could take them. Easily," Geno replied.

"But we wouldn't enter without Gabe. It wouldn't be right," Jeb added.

Gator clenched his teeth as Haslow leaned over the bar to whisper to Alana. The place was getting louder, and it was obvious she couldn't hear him as she leaned closer and closed her eyes. Gator watched her eyes pop open, and her face turned a nice shade of red. She shook her head and laughed.

"I don't think we're serving that here," she told him, and he chuckled and continued to try and talk with her. She listened as his buddies joined in. Jake, Vincent, and even Tito flirted with her.

She walked away after making their drinks and headed back toward Gator and his friends. Gator locked gazes with Haslow as his and his team's eyes watched Alana's ass.

As soon as Haslow's eyes landed on Gator's, his expression changed. He lifted his mug of beer and gave a smirk. Gator disliked that asshole. So did the others.

"Need some refills, gentlemen?" Alana asked, and before he could reply Geno was curling his finger toward Alana, asking her to come closer.

She pulled her bottom lip between her teeth as she leaned forward, her body language different than when Haslow was close to her and whispering into her ear.

Geno reached up and tugged on her hair, letting his hand move along the back of her neck under her hair. He said something to her, and her face instantly reddened. Then she turned slightly and locked gazes with Gator. Gator was still angry over Haslow's flirtatious moves that he didn't break his expression, and before he thought to give Alana a nicer expression, she began to move back.

Her breasts looked incredible in the top she wore, and he could see the blotchiness on her chest. Geno got to her.

"Let me refill those beers for you," Alana told Geno, who lifted the almost empty beer glass to his lips, never letting his eyes leave Alana's.

Gator watched Alana as she filled each new mug with cold beer from the tap. The muscles in her arms flexed, and he could see the definition in her shoulders and along her neck. She handed Geno a mug first then him and then Jeb.

Then she moved on to serve some more drinks.

"What the hell did you say to her?" Jeb asked Geno before Gator could.

"Just warning her about those assholes at the end of the bar."

"It looked like you told her something else," Gator replied.

"I might have mentioned that we're the jealous types, and that if she let any other man whisper into her ear, that you were going to toss them out on their asses, just like you did the first set of guys."

Gator cracked a smile. "And she didn't tell you to fuck off?"

Geno held his steady expression, his eyes still on Alana.

"I think she completely understood what I was implying."

* * * *

Alana was practically shaking. She was trying to act unaffected by Geno, Jeb, and Gator, but it seemed she was totally attracted to the three men, and they felt the same way. How fucking complicated was this situation? She couldn't flirt back or accept their advances. They were Gabe's team members. Besides that, she wasn't over Gabe. She still loved him and thought constantly about how she could get through to him.

But this wasn't right. They probably flirted with her, and Geno had said what he did to make her think they cared and were interested, because really they felt obligated to watch over her. But why? Gabe had made his position clear. *He wants to be dead to me.*

"Hey, beautiful, you ought to stay down here where the real men are. Come on over here and talk to us," the guy who'd introduced himself earlier as Haslow told her.

She raised one eyebrow and gave him the once-over.

"I think the place is filled with real men. Maybe even a few jerks," she replied.

His buddies chuckled, but Haslow got annoyed.

"Those assholes badmouthing me down there?" he asked then looked that way.

She glanced over and saw the intense expressions on Geno's, Gator's and Jeb's faces. She gulped. She didn't need to cause a bar fight. She'd lose her job.

"No, they were saying the complete opposite. Something about you being good men. Real upstanding citizens. So do you need another round?"

Haslow nodded and then lifted the mug of beer toward Gator and the guys. Alana had to hide her chuckle. Hopefully she'd just diffused a potential situation.

It had been a very busy night. She didn't even want to think about tomorrow as the bar got less and less crowded and Haslow and his friends, who turned out to be nice guys, left. Alana looked down toward the end of the bar and the table filled with stragglers as she cleaned up along with Garrett and Mike. She could see Geno, Jeb, Gator, and Garrett's two brothers, Wes and Gunner, talking. A few other men were there too. They were joking around, and every so often Jeb, Gator, or Geno would look up as if they were watching over her. She felt on edge and nervous. Just thinking about entertaining an attraction to another man besides Gabe made her panic. But to know his good friends, his roommates, and team members were attracted to her, and she to them, made her feel like throwing up.

"You did fantastic tonight. A lot of the regulars complimented your drink making skills. Especially those specialty martinis and margaritas," Garrett told her as they finished up.

"Thank you. I was a bit rusty."

"Well, you can work on sharpening your skills tomorrow night."

"What do you mean? Isn't Stella coming back?"

"She's not reliable, as you could tell. We were trying to help a family friend out, but it isn't working. Besides, you're a better bartender, have a hell of a lot better personality, and you've got the touch with the patrons. They liked you. Some more than others." He nodded toward the table of men as he wiped out the inside of another glass.

She felt her cheeks warm.

"Well, I'm just trying to make a living. Not really interested in making new friends."

Garrett raised one eyebrow at her.

"There's always room for new friends, Alana. I can vouch for those guys. Geno, Jeb, and Gator are good men. Tough Marines who hardly ever come in here or stay this late. Their other roommates, Jaxon and Gabe, are good men too. Just not real sociable types.

She swallowed hard at the mention of Gabe's name. It made her chest ache.

"Well, I appreciate the info, but as I said, I'm not looking to make new friends. Thank you for asking me to bartend again."

"Not just again, doll. As a new position. My dad already has my mom looking for two replacement waitresses. So welcome to the elite group of special bartenders here at Casper's. Here. This is your share of the tips tonight."

She took the envelope from Garrett and felt how thick it was. She figured there were a lot of dollar bills, but as she opened it up, she was shocked. There were big bills too.

"Like I said, you did great tonight. It was very crowded. You'll make a lot more than you would have made waitressing."

She smiled.

"Thank you so much. This will be a great help. Is it always so busy?" She reached under the bar for her backpack and light sweater.

"For the most part. Tomorrow night might be even more crowded. This is the last weekend of the county fair, so a lot of people will be here tomorrow night. Sunday is the final day."

"Oh, I thought I saw some signs about that on my way in from Tranquility. Where is it located?" She pulled her sweater on.

Garrett gave her directions and told her that he, his brothers, and their wife, Gia, would be attending on Sunday.

"Maybe you want to go with us?" he asked.

"I'll think about it. Thanks." She said goodnight and had started walking around the bar when she heard chairs scraping against the floor. She looked up and saw Gator, Gabe, and Jeb standing up and shaking hands with the other men. It was as though they were leaving with her, and she felt panicked.

"We'll walk you out, Alana," Gabe told her.

"Oh you don't have to. Stay and enjoy the night with your friends," she replied.

Gator gave her a firm expression. "We were waiting on you," he said, and boy, did those words do a number to her body.

Jeb held the door open, and she waved to the other guys who looked smug at the show of possession from Gator, Jeb, and Geno.

As they exited, she felt the cool night air, and it was nice against her heated skin.

"It's a little chilly. You should button that sweater up," Jeb told her as he squeezed her shoulders.

"It feels great. I was so hot in there tonight."

"You looked hot in there too," Geno replied as she got to her car and turned to face him. She was shocked at his comment.

Locking gazes with the very tall, muscular man intimidated her. He stood right in front of her, and Gator and Jeb stood on either side. They surrounded her, and she felt her pussy clench. God, this was really bad. Really, really bad.

"Listen, I think I should tell you that I don't need looking after. I know you must feel compelled to keep an eye on me, but it isn't necessary. I can take care of myself." She turned to open the car door, but Geno pressed his hand over it, stopping her. She faced the car and could feel the heat of his large, sexy body against her hip and ass.

"Darlin', we are not watching over you because we feel obligated to do so. We're here because we want to be. We want to get to know you better."

She turned around to face him. Them. "No. It's not a good idea."

Geno stepped closer and cupped her cheek and neck with his warm hand.

"Whether we like it or not, it's happening."

She shook her head.

"It can't. I can't. I'm sorry," she said, but he leaned closer, tilted her head up toward him, and touched his lips to hers.

It felt so good to be kissed by a man again. Strong, warm, passionate lips against her more delicate mouth. The feel of him pressing closer and tasting her brought on a surge of emotions. His masculinity, the scent of his cologne, the feeling of being protected by a man consumed her, and then came images of Gabe.

She pulled back, the tears instantly sparking in her eyes.

"Alana?"

She shook her head.

"It isn't fair. I can't do this. You don't seem to understand." She pressed her hands against Geno's chest. Gator and Jeb placed their hands on her shoulders.

"We do understand. You still love Gabe," Gator whispered.

"Despite what you might think, I never dated anyone else. I never kissed anyone else. To kiss you, and to feel something, is too much. I'm sorry. I'm not ready for this."

She turned around and opened the car door. The men stepped back, but Geno took her hand. He brought it to his lips as she paused before getting into her car.

"Take your time, Alana. We're not going anywhere. This isn't an attraction any of us can ignore or simply walk away from."

"I'm afraid that's exactly the right thing to do." She pulled away, got into her car, and started the engine. She wouldn't look at them as she put the car in drive and slowly pulled out of the parking spot. She couldn't look at them and wish for things to be different, to let this attraction happen. She needed to distance herself from thoughts of them and Gabe. That was the point of moving out of Scrantonville. But it seemed God was into playing tricks on her. With these guys around, she would never get Gabe out of her head. Ever.

Chapter 2

Gabe sat on the back porch and stared out into the woods. Jaxon sat on the chair with his feet up on the porch railing. The others had gotten in late last night. It seemed something interested them in town the last several days.

"It's going to be a nice day for the fair. The last one before they head out of town," Jaxon told him.

Gabe didn't really give a shit about fairs, parties, social gatherings, or anything else. His leg throbbed, his head hurt, and he couldn't sleep. Not even the meds from the local doctor helped him sleep. Not with his mind on Alana.

"There'll be something else in Salvation next weekend and the next and so forth. There's always something being celebrated," Gabe said, sounding bitter to his own ears. He was filled with hatred, anger, and felt as though his heart was hollow. Except seeing Alana had given him a reaction he'd thought he buried.

"That's because towns like Salvation, and eventually Tranquility too, like to celebrate life and bring people together."

"Fuck that," he practically spat.

"You're really full of piss and vinegar this morning. Didn't get enough sleep?"

"Never fucking do anymore. A wink here and there. Not much the last few days."

"Thinking about anything in particular? Or maybe someone in particular?" Jaxon pushed, and Gabe turned toward him.

Jaxon had been their leader in the Marines. Even as civilians now, Gabe looked to him for direction, for support, and even comfort. God knows if Gabe had gone off and tried living off the land and disappearing, he would have taken his own life.

"Just aching, that's all," he lied.

Jaxon was silent a moment, and Gabe thought he was clear of any potential discussion. But no such luck.

"Why didn't you tell us about Alana?"

He felt his chest tighten, and the emotions he was trying so hard to bury jumped forward, and he quickly suppressed them.

"Nothing to tell."

"Didn't seem so from her reaction to seeing you."

"She thought I was dead. That was the plan."

"You reacted too."

He clenched his teeth. "Don't know what you mean."

"Fuck that shit. You don't know what I mean. I fucking saw it. I saw your eyes widen and excitement fill them, and then you went straight-faced. You love her."

"Used to, but it's over."

"She still loves you."

"She'll get over it. Don't let her sweetness fool ya."

"Don't even try that shit with me. You've never been a man to put a woman, or any other person, down. You're a goddamn Marine. Start fucking acting like one."

"What's that supposed to mean?"

"It means tell the fucking truth. We've all been pussyfooting around why you're so compelled to not move on and adapt to civilian life. Why you're depressed, angry all the time, and hurtful in your comments. The rest of us have adapted. Why can't you?"

"Because of this." He slapped the upper part of his pants over his thigh. He lifted the cane and slammed it against the wooden railing of the porch.

"So you have a war injury and need a cane. Who cares?"

"I do."

"Well, she wouldn't care."

"How the fuck would you know that? You don't know her. She would act fine with it, but the moment she laid eyes on the gaping hole in my leg and the scars and welts, she would turn away. I'm not even fucking whole anymore. She's perfection."

"She sure the fuck is."

Gabe looked up to see Geno in the doorway with a cup of coffee.

Gabe exhaled and leaned back in his chair.

"She is perfect. She's beautiful, sweet, has one hell of a body, never mind a great personality. And we weren't the only ones to notice her last night," Geno told him.

Gabe swung around to look at him. His chest tightened, and his heart ached. He fucking loved Alana with all his heart, but she deserved better.

"You were with her?"

Geno smirked as he set the mug down and looked out over the porch railing.

"If I thought she would have accepted, then I would have invited her to come home with us last night."

Gabe reached out and grabbed his arm. He clenched his teeth and saw fucking red.

"You want to fuck her?"

"What man in his right mind would give up a fine piece of ass like that, all ready for the taking?"

Gabe tried jumping up but stumbled and grabbed onto the arm of the chair. He felt about ready to explode.

"You son of a bitch. She isn't like that. You stay the fuck away from her."

Gabe saw Geno look at Jaxon and smirk. Then he noticed Gator and Jeb in the doorway, looking serious.

"I told you he still loves her. He's just feeling sorry for himself," Geno said, and Gabe realized what they had done. They'd made him confess his true feelings. He fell back into the seat and ran his hands over his face.

"So do you want to hear about the guys who hit on your girlfriend last night and how you weren't there to protect her?" Jeb asked, now joining in this attack.

"No. I don't care. She's not my girlfriend."

"So you won't mind if the four of us make a move and make her ours then?" Geno asked, and Gabe shot a look from him to Jaxon. Jaxon didn't look surprised. He looked intense.

"You want to share my girlfriend?" Gabe said the words, and he was shocked at the mix of jealousy, anger, and arousal he felt. These were his brothers in arms, his team, and he would give his life for them. What were they up to?

"She's not your girlfriend. You gave up that right when you pretended to be dead," Jeb snapped at him.

"You don't understand. You don't get it," Gabe told him.

"I don't understand? No. I think it's you who doesn't understand. She still loves you," Jeb said.

"But she's attracted to the four of us as well, and we're attracted to her," Gator told him next.

"What are you trying to tell me? You want to fight over her? She'll pick any of you over me. You're all whole, and I'm way past fucked up."

"Maybe in your head because you're so busy feeling sorry for yourself and assuming that the people who love you would turn their backs on you and pity you," Jeb said.

"They would. I don't need their pity. I don't need to stick a beautiful woman like Alana with a man who can't even walk without a cane."

"I don't think Alana gives a shit about any of that," Jaxon told him.

"You don't know," Gabe said, feeling his anger building again. His own team wanted to sleep with Alana. His woman and they wanted her. But she wasn't his woman. He'd given that right up when he decided not to return home. He looked at his team, his brothers, and could see all they had to offer Alana. Their protection, their commitment, their perfection. They were all big men, and Alana was feminine and petite. She had grown her brown hair longer, and her green eyes had never looked so green. They had shined that day at the estate sale. Glistened with tears. Tears and pain he caused her. His team would make her happy. His team was a group of perfect men.

"Don't look at us like that," Jaxon exclaimed.

"Like what?"

"Like you think we're better than you because we don't have the depth of scars you have," Jeb told him.

"We all have scars, physical, mental. But we push through and don't allow them to rule our thoughts," Gator said.

"Well then, I guess you're better than I am."

"Come on, Gabe. Get your head out of your ass and think about this, will ya?" Jaxon said.

"I want nothing to do with this. With Alana. It's over. Do whatever you want." He stood up and grabbed the cane tight.

"You're telling us to pursue our attraction to her and that you don't want to be part of this?" Geno asked him.

He swallowed hard. His saliva felt like poison going down his throat. He so badly wanted to be a part of it. He needed them beside him to get through being close to Alana. But how could he admit such weakness to men who obviously were way stronger in every aspect than he was?

"Do whatever you want with her. I don't care. Just leave me out of it." He walked off the porch and into the house. He heard their curses and the heated tones of their voices as they cursed his attitude and his lack of a heart. But that was just it. He didn't have a heart. His heart was hollow inside. He never should have made it out of Iraq alive.

* * * *

"So you're telling me that she feels the same attraction, but she hasn't kissed or been with any other man than Gabe?" Jaxon asked them, and Geno, Gator, and Jeb filled him in on everything that happened last night. Jaxon was shocked. He was also annoyed that Haslow and his friends had been hitting on Alana. They would need to nip that in the bud pretty damn fast.

"So you're serious? You want to pursue Alana? You want us to share her if she's willing?" Jaxon asked, feeling his heart beat faster and tightness fill his chest.

"We weren't too sure until last night," Geno replied.

"He kissed her," Jeb told Jaxon, and Jaxon's eyes widened.

"She kissed me back, but then she pulled away. She thought of Gabe. I just know it. She still loves him," Geno told Jaxon.

"Then how could you guys consider this type of relationship?"

"Because the attraction is there. This could work. This could bring Gabe and the rest of us together the way we were before. He needs her, and he needs us. I think this type of relationship can serve all of us, including Alana," Gator told him.

"Are you certain it's best for Alana too? I've thought about my own attraction to her, and honestly, I'm afraid it might cause a wedge between Gabe and me," Jaxon admitted.

"I think it's exactly what she needs," Geno told them. "It's what Gabe needs. That push to remember why he was out there fighting, and that there are people who care about him. For Alana, hell, she lives all alone. She admitted to not kissing any other man since Gabe. We can help heal her and protect her so she's never alone again. They'll always be one of us with her at all times. She'll know she has Gabe and all of us to take care of her and be here for her. We've seen these relationship work for men just like us, and for similar reasons. There's not much we do alone anymore. This is a great idea."

"And Alana? How will we explain our intentions?" Jaxon asked.

"Slowly and diligently. You weren't there last night. We're not the only men interested in getting to know Alana. In fact, we're heading to the fair by noontime. Alana should be going there with Garrett, Gunner, Wes, and Gia," Gator told him.

"And Gabe?" Jeb asked.

"We'll bring him along, but he's on his own. This is something he has to learn to handle, and it's his decision to join us or to let Alana move on," Geno said, and they all agreed before they headed into the house to get ready.

* * * *

Alana stood on the porch, and an eerie feeling filled her belly. It was sudden. A sensation like she was being watched. She squinted her eyes toward the woods, as if that might help her see more clearly. But no such luck. It seemed her eyes were playing tricks on her. For every movement of a branch or a tree, she thought she saw a shadow of someone.

But her father had trained her well. Being the daughter of a Marine, she'd learned early how to shoot guns and be ready for the unexpected. She had a lot of friends whose fathers or mothers were cops, and they were just as well trained. Deciding that it was better to go back inside to wait for Gia and the guys to get there, she stood up and saw the movement in the corner of her eye. Sure as shit, there was someone out there.

Her heart pounded, and she hurried inside to where her gun was. The sound of banging on the door made her scream aloud, and she held the gun steady in her hands.

"Who is it?" she yelled.

"Alana, it's Gia. Are you okay?"

Alana lowered the gun and sighed in relief. She quickly unlocked the door and opened it.

Gia looked at her face and then the gun in her hand.

"What's wrong?" Gia asked as Garrett, Gunner, and Wes hurried up the walkway.

"I was out back on the porch waiting, and I thought I saw someone watching me. As I got up to go inside because I felt creepy, I saw him in the woods."

"Jesus," Wes said.

"We'll go check it out. You get inside and wait for us," Gunner said, and he and Garrett headed around the house.

Alana put the safety on her gun and then walked over to the cabinet.

"You got yourself a damn arsenal, woman. You know how to use all those guns?" Wes asked, moving closer.

"Of course I do. Trained by one of the best."

"What, a cop?" Wes asked.

"No. Marine."

Wes looked at Gia, and Alana noticed the exchange.

"You talking about Gabe Weathers?"

She shook her head and felt the tightness in her chest. She was still shaking with concern over the strange man in the woods watching her.

"My daddy," she told Wes then closed the cabinet.

"Your father was a Marine, huh? Something else we have in common, Alana, besides knowing how to make a mean martini," Wes teased.

The front door opened, and Alana jumped. Garrett and Gunner were there.

"Was definitely someone out there. Saw some boot prints. They're not there now. Did you get a good look at the guy?" Gunner asked her, and Alana shook her head.

"He was camouflaged by the trees."

"She's got herself a nice arsenal of weapons here, Gunner, and she knows how to use them," Wes told his brother.

Gunner walked over and nodded toward the case on the wall. Alana opened it up. He whistled.

"You know how to use all these?"

She lifted one eyebrow at him.

"Well, I don't expect to have to come out here and clean up a mess when you pull something out and shoot the shit out of some guy."

"If that guy breaks into my home, then I guess that's a possibility."

He chuckled. "Let's hope not. I'll call the local deputy here in Tranquility. Maybe he can do some drive-bys and look into who walks around those woods out back. I'm sure it was just some nosey hiker or something," he said, obviously trying to ease her mind.

"I hope so too," she whispered, and then she went to grab her sweater and her backpack. She locked the back door and rechecked the windows too. They all seemed to recheck what she just checked, which reiterated that they felt the guy in the woods was no nosy hiker.

They headed out, and Alana didn't want to think about coming home to the dark, empty cottage alone. But she wouldn't act like a chicken. She was used to being alone and not relying on a man. That was one thing she was forced to live without. The protection of a man like Gabe.

* * * *

"That's no way to win a woman's heart, friend," Gunner told Jaxon as Jaxon watched Alana while she talked to two cowboys. They were being gentleman and all, but that possessive feeling was getting in the way of Jaxon's rational attitude.

"What do you mean?" he asked Gunner.

"That mean, nasty puss you got plastered on your face. Scare the heck out of kids, never mind one very young, attractive, green-eyed woman."

Jaxon glanced at Gunner. "Can't help it. She shouldn't be talking to any of those men."

"If you think she should be talking to you, or one of your team members, then you guys should make a move."

"How the hell can we?"

"Gabe will come around. He's got to work through his emotions and all the hell he went through."

"I can't condone starting a complex relationship like this with myself and my team without Gabe on board."

"Well, that's stupid. Gabe will figure his shit out. He hasn't taken his eyes off of her either."

"That's another thing. Alana can't even look at Gabe without filling up with tears."

"She loves him still, but she has feelings for you guys as well, right?"

"Seems that way. Still doesn't make this an ideal beginning to a potential love affair."

"A love affair, huh?" Gunner asked and chuckled low. Jaxon didn't cut a smile.

They were silent a few moments, and then Gunner changed the subject.

Jaxon was grateful until he heard the direction the conversation was headed.

"Did you catch the guy?" Jaxon asked, standing straighter then looking for Alana again. Gia was walking with her toward the vendors.

"No. But Alana was smart. She got inside, she locked up the doors, and she grabbed her gun."

"Her gun?"

"She's got herself an arsenal."

"She could hurt herself."

"Not likely considering what Wes told me."

"Which was what?"

"She told him she was trained by a Marine."

"Gabe," Jaxon whispered and then looked to see where he was, but he had disappeared.

"Nope. Her father."

"Her dad was a jarhead?" Jaxon asked, both surprised and intrigued.

"Sure was. But I still called it into the department in Tranquility. Deputy Peters said he'd personally look into it."

"Fuck. I bet he will. He'll call his cousin, Vincent. He, Haslow, Tito, and the bunch will be knocking on Alana's door volunteering to be her personal bodyguards." That just concerned Jaxon more, especially since Gator had told him how Haslow and his team were flirting with Alana.

"We plan on walking her inside tonight and checking things out before we leave her alone there for the night."

"We can do that. I won't be able to rest tonight unless I know personally that she's okay."

"Understandable. But that's only if Alana says she's okay with it. Deanna would have my ass if I didn't look out for her with all this shit Alana's going through. Deanna still hasn't informed Gabe's parents that he's alive and well."

"Hopefully, he'll get over that and tell them himself one day real soon."

"Hopefully."

Jaxon heard Gia call his name, and then she waved for him to come on over and join them. Jaxon watched as Alana locked gazes with Jaxon and then turned away. She jumped as Jeb snuck up behind her, smiling.

Now he would worry about some Peeping Tom watching Alana. There was no way she was going home alone. In fact, she might just have an overnight guest, even if he had to sleep on her couch.

* * * *

"You scared me." Alana told Jeb as he appeared out of nowhere. He held her arms and rubbed them. "Sorry, doll. I didn't mean to."

She gulped as he leaned down and kissed her cheek.

"Are you having fun?" he asked then ran one hand down her arm to her hand and clasped their fingers together.

At first she felt as though she should pull away. She was still feeling edgy from earlier at her cottage. But now, with the feel of Jeb's much-larger hand holding her small one, she felt instantly safe.

As they walked around the fair looking at different items the vendors were selling, she leaned closer. She missed holding hands with a man and just walking around enjoying the time together. But her insecurities and her concern over Gabe's reaction had her putting on the brakes.

She stopped and pulled from Jeb and walked closer to one of the vendor tables. She reached for the first thing she saw, a series of bracelets, some with charms and others just plain silver or gold.

The warm, male hand on her waist made her begin to shake. There were so many nights she longed to be held in bed. Longed for Gabe, for that ability a man had to make a woman feel safe, content, and loved. But it was wrong to have an attraction to the men in Gabe's team, his roommates, his fellow Marines. Besides, she never really saw herself getting involved in a ménage relationship. Not that she was against them. She just never expected to have such a reaction to multiple men at once. She was so afraid of getting close to anyone out of the fear of losing them that it seemed safer, and wiser, to keep her distance.

Jeb's hand caressed down her wrist and over the bracelet she held in her hand. He whispered over her shoulder, pressing his body closer to hers. "That one is pretty."

She eased back to feel him snuggle against her body. His hand on her waist slid along to her belly in a possessive manner. She felt feminine, petite, and most definitely aroused.

Alana warned herself to gain some control here. She was just thinking how wrong this was to like Gabe's friends, perhaps even lust for them, and now she was taking every opportunity to feel Jeb against her.

"I don't know," she whispered as she continued to look at the bracelets. She could feel his hips against her ass. Their significant difference in sizes was arousing too. She felt oversensitive to everything, including the rough texture of his jeans, the hardness of his thighs, the thick, masculinity of his hands on her body. It was all hitting her, making her palms sweat, her heart race, and anxiety fill her belly.

"What do you think about this one?" Jeb asked, holding up a nice silver bracelet with a dangling angel charm surrounded by three silver balls on each side.

"It suits you," he told her.

"That is very pretty. It's feminine and petite, juts like you," the woman behind the table told them.

Alana smiled at the woman as Jeb placed it on Alana's wrist.

"How much is it?" Alana asked.

"Twenty," the woman replied, but before Alana could hand over her money, Jaxon was there giving the twenty-dollar bill to the woman.

Jeb smiled.

"Isn't it perfect?" Jeb asked Jaxon.

Jaxon lifted Alana's hand up but held her gaze, instead of checking out the bracelet.

"She is perfect." He winked, and Alana blushed.

"Jaxon, please."

"Come on. Let's continue to look around."

Jaxon placed his hands on her shoulders, and she was grateful he didn't take her hand. She might do something stupid like hug him. But as they walked through the fair and around the vendors, she caught sight of the others, including Gabe sitting at a large table. Her heart began to pound again, this time bringing instant sickness and fear.

How can I sit near by Gabe and act like he doesn't exist and like we weren't in love? How can I pretend to be friendly when all I want to do is scream and cry, yell at him and demand he come back to me and be the man I remember? How can he just give up on us and what we had? Why doesn't he love me? How can he just ignore me and not want to hold me like I've longed to hold him? God help me get through this. God, I can't do this.

She paused three tables away from where they all sat.

"I'm sorry. I need to use the lady's room. I'll meet you after," she told Jeb and Jaxon.

Jaxon gave her that look. An expression a commander gives a soldier when he knows he's up to something.

"I'll walk with you," Jeb offered.

"No. I'll be fine. Go with your friends, and I'll be back."

He gave her a knowing smile and then ran his knuckles gently against her cheek.

"Hurry back," Jeb said, and she nodded, turned away, and instantly felt the sickness lessen.

As she quickly headed toward the center of the fairgrounds, where there was a building with restrooms and information, she turned to her right and bumped into someone.

The man grabbed her by her waist and stared right into her eyes.

His eyes were dark, angry, and definitely creepy, and she stepped back, but he didn't release her.

"I'm so sorry. I didn't see you," he said to her.

"That's okay. It was my fault too."

"Have I seen you before?" he asked her, releasing his hold but still in her space.

She pushed a strand of hair behind her ear.

"No, I don't think so."

"Well, you look familiar. I would remember such a pretty face."

She thought the man was kind of strange, especially the way he looked her body over and even eyed her breasts. She knew she was well endowed, but he was blatantly staring.

"Sorry again. Enjoy the fair." She turned to go, but he reached out and gripped her wrist.

She gasped and debated about slugging him, making a counter move, or just yelling and making a scene. But he must have realized what he had done because he quickly released her wrist.

"The clothing boutique in Tranquility. That's where we met."

She shook her head.

"I don't think so," she replied and held his gaze.

"Yes, a little over two weeks ago, your first day on the job, and I couldn't find the right size shirt. You helped me." As he spoke, his eyes sparkled, and again she felt this creepy sensation.

"Well, I'm sorry that I don't remember you. I'm glad that I was able to help you."

"Do you like working there, or do you like working at Casper's better?"

Instantly, she went on alert. How did this man know she worked at Casper's? Was he following her or something?

"How did you—"

"Oh, I go there with friends and saw you working yesterday. You're a hard worker. That's impressive."

He looked at her arms, her shoulders, and body. She needed to walk away. How many times over the years had weird men hit on her or tried flirting and she got a funny sensation? It was a gut instinct that she needed to respect and listen to.

"Well, I'm sorry, but I need to go. I'm meeting friends."

His expression changed to an angry one as he looked over his shoulder and back toward the tables where the men sat. Again, she couldn't help but wonder if the man was watching her. How strange.

"I'll see you around then." She nodded, turned, and hurried toward the building. But before she entered, she looked over her shoulder and saw the man watching her. But then he nodded and smiled before he started walking away.

That guy was definitely a little weird. She headed inside, hoping to waste more time and gather the strength she needed to face Gabe and his roommates.

* * * *

"Are you kidding me? What is Gunner going to do? What about Deputy Peters?" Gabe asked Jaxon as he told them about what happened at Alana's house when Gunner and the guys got there earlier to pick her up.

Gabe was instantly upset and angry. Alana was gorgeous. It was taking so much will and fight to not hold her, touch her, hell, kiss her and feel her in his arms. But he couldn't do that to her. She shouldn't have to settle for a man like him. Maybe letting his friends care for her would at least allow him to know she was safe and secure.

"Well, the thing is, Peters said he would personally take care of driving by her place and checking on things," Jaxon told them.

"Vincent and those guys hit on Alana the other night at Casper's. Now his cousin, the deputy, wants to watch over her? I think fucking not," Gator stated firmly, his fists clenched.

Gabe looked at him and then at Jeb, Geno, and Jaxon. They all already cared a lot about Alana. She would be safest with them.

"What are you going to do about this?" Gabe asked Jaxon.

Jaxon raised one eyebrow up at him.

"Me? How about us, as a team, Gabe? You know you care about her. Hell, you haven't been able to take your eyes off of her," Jaxon told him.

"She's a beautiful woman," Gabe whispered, his heart aching.

"She was yours, and could still be yours and ours, if you would get your head out of your ass about not being good enough for her," Geno told Gabe.

"Fuck you."

"No, fuck you," Geno said, and Gabe stood up.

"I don't need this. Just protect her. That's all I need to know about any of this plan you all have." He grabbed his cane and began to walk away. As he headed around the corner, he spotted Alana. She was talking to Vincent, deputy Will Peters' cousin.

A deep, angry, jealous feeling filled him as he watched Vincent touch her hand and lift her wrist up to look at some bracelet she wore. How dare the fucker touch her? It seemed she had an effect on every man around her, and they all felt compelled to be close to her. She was his girlfriend. He was the first man to ever make love to her. He was shocked that thought hit his brain because then came the thought of another man having her. He saw red just thinking of Vincent touching her body and making her moan in pleasure. But when he thought of himself loving her, he felt incapable, weak, and not whole. He would need his brothers, his team, to make her his woman again. That thought struck him so hard that he felt the tears reach his eyes and his belly ache with the realization.

They all needed one another here, and without them, he would always feel not good enough. But with his team, with all of them claiming Alana as their woman, then he could feel as though there was a chance at a little bit of happiness with the woman he'd fought so hard to live for.

* * * *

"So my cousin is going to be doing some drive-bys even at night. So don't be too concerned if you see some lights and vehicles near the woods," Vincent told her.

"That's very kind of him. I'm sure it's nothing to worry about."

Vincent reached up and gently glided a strand of her hair between his fingers.

"You should always take precautions anyway. In fact, we should exchange numbers so, if you ever need anything, I can get to your place fast," he told her.

"I don't think she'll be needing that, Vincent."

Alana swung her head around to see Gabe, and she nearly lost her balance. She hadn't expected him to show up or to interrupt this conversation. By the way he had been acting and his whole dead-to-the-world attitude, she was floored.

"Gabe. How are you doing?" Vincent asked him and reached out his hand to shake Gabe's.

Gabe was a gentleman and did so, and Vincent seemed to look at Gabe as if he felt sorry for him. Something clicked inside of Alana's head.

"I was just being neighborly and letting Alana know that she has a friend nearby she can call if she ever needs anything." Vincent winked at Alana.

"Yeah, well, she has my buddies, and they'll be watching over her. In fact, we were waiting for her to come back to the tables for lunch. So if you don't mind…" Gabe said to Vincent.

"I'll see you in town, Alana, or maybe at Casper's next week. Friday and Saturday are your nights, right?"

"Yes. I'll see you around, and thank your cousin for me please."

"I'm sure he'll be by your place. You can thank him yourself."

She smiled as he walked away. Vincent was a very nice guy. A lot nicer than when he had a few too many drinks in him.

"I don't want you talking to him. He'll take it the wrong way and think you're interested."

She shot a look at Gabe. He was so big and tall that her head tilted back to nearly her shoulders. "You don't want me talking to him? Really? Why would you even care who I talk to? You're dead to me, remember?" she said in anger and began to walk away.

He grabbed her arm and held her close. Their bodies pressed together, and she gasped. This was how it always was with them. This intense connection, this desire and need so overwhelming they had to have one another and be close.

He immediately stepped back, recomposed himself, and looked away from her then back.

The bastard. How the hell can he do that? He had to have felt what I felt. Why was he trying so hard to push me away? Why am I even here talking to him? Because I still love him. Fudge!

"He's not right for you. Besides, I said I was dead and had my reasons for doing that."

"Like what kind of reasons?" she asked him as she tried to look into his dark eyes and see something, anything that could give her a hint to his way of thinking right now.

"I'm not going to talk about it. It doesn't matter."

"Well, it matters to me. It matters to your parents and all the people in Scrantonville who think you're still dead."

"Alana, don't push me. I have my reasons."

"So you keep telling me. How can you stand there and expect me to not be angry with you? To not break down and cry because of everything I went through thinking you were dead this entire time?"

"What you went through? What about what I went through? Have you turned into such a self-centered princess?"

She didn't think twice as she shoved at his chest. He stumbled back. She felt a shot of guilt, but he recovered, and she was angry all over again.

She pointed at her chest. "*I'm* the same person. I haven't changed at all, so apparently if you can call me a self-centered princess, then you never really knew me, Gabe. That hurts." She turned and began walking away.

"Alana, wait."

He placed his hand on her shoulder from behind, and she stopped dead in her tracks. Her muscles tightened, and then that warm, deep feeling filtered through her skin and her bones. She longed to feel his touch. She'd begged God every night for Gabe's return home from the service. She squeezed her eyes tight and pleaded to just be able to feel Gabe's touch again. To feel his big, strong, muscular arms surround her.

She hadn't even realized he was walking with her and that they wound up by a tree guarded by leaves and onlookers. Tears streamed down her cheeks, and a sob arose from deep in her gut. Then Gabe turned her around and hugged her tight. She lost it. She sobbed as the memories of all those lonely, sad days and nights filtered through her mind, making her numb and exhausted.

* * * *

Gabe felt his eyes well up with tears and his heart fill with emotion. He inhaled Alana's shampoo and the scent of her perfume. He squeezed her petite frame against his body and felt his cock instantly harden with thoughts of making love to her and that utter complete sensation when their two bodies were joined so intimately.

Then came the fear, the terror of not being able to be the man she needed, the one she deserved. He thought about the things he'd witnessed and the actions he'd partaken in. He was a changed man. He was a damaged, violent man who should have died out in that godforsaken dessert or in one of the trenches out by the roadways.

He felt meaningless, and he felt dirty, like some wild, untamed beast that could hurt Alana in the midst of one of his episodes.

"Alana, don't cry. I'm sure this is upsetting. But you need to do as I ask. It's what's right for you."

She pulled back and looked up at him. Her gorgeous green eyes were sparkling with tears clinging to her thick, long eyelashes. Her lips were full and wet, and he wanted to kiss her, get lost in every aspect of Alana.

"What's right for me? How would you know what's right for me?"

"Because I know you. I know you put everyone first in all you do. I know you've suffered over the last few years thinking that I was dead."

"Suffered?" She sniffled. "They were the worst three years of my life. If I hadn't moved out of Scrantonville to get out from under the depression and constant reminders of my love for you, then I never would have found you. I would still be thinking that you were dead. I would still be all alone."

He cupped her cheeks.

"But you're not alone anymore. Jaxon, Geno, Gator, and Jeb want you." He took a deep breath and released it, realizing it hurt to say this and to push her away and toward his team. But they would make her happy. They were good, whole men who would commit to only her.

"And what about you, Gabe? Don't you want me anymore?" she asked as another tear rolled down her cheek.

It was torture to see her like this, to know that he loved her but could not have her or tell her.

"No. I don't want you. But they do, and they'll treat you right and make you happy."

She shook her head and pulled back. She used her sleeve to wipe the tears from her eyes, and she stood straighter. She was the daughter of a Marine. She wasn't weak. She was a soldier in so many ways.

"Well, that's not really your decision, Gabe." She looked away from him. A glance in that direction and he could see the concerned faces as his friends drew closer.

She held his gaze, and he nearly gulped under her perusal.

"Do you know what I think? I think you're scared shitless. I think you've given up on yourself and your capabilities, and you know what? I still love you, and there's not a damn thing you can say or do to make me not love you. So what I suggest is that you wake up and snap out of whatever screwed-up shit you've trained your brain to believe. I'm living in Tranquility now, and I'll talk to any man or men I want to and not just the ones you push me toward."

She stormed off, and Gabe stood there watching her leave. He felt enraged, angry, and then he felt disgusted with himself. He was being a heartless bastard. It was obvious that she still loved him the way he still loved her.

He ran his fingers through his hair. *I can't bring her down. I'm not good enough for her.*

"What's going on? What did you say to Alana?" Jaxon demanded to know.

"Nothing. We were talking."

"Talking my ass. She was crying. What the fuck, Gabe?" Gator gave Gabe's shoulder a shove, and then he stormed off in the direction Alana had gone.

"What is your fucking problem? Why do you find it necessary to keep hurting her?" Jeb asked Gabe as he stared at him with his fists by his sides. His buddies, his team members all looked ready to kill him.

"What? I'm not intentionally hurting her."

"Then why follow her if you didn't mean to upset her?" Geno asked this time.

"I wanted to try to talk with her, and then I saw her with Vincent."

"Vincent?" Geno asked and then looked furious and jealous all at once. Gabe had felt the same way but had denied it.

"I interrupted them. He was telling her she could call him any time she needed him and that his cousin was going to take extra care to watch over her and the cottage."

"Fucking asshole." Geno practically spat his words.

"What did you do?" Jaxon asked.

"I told him that we had her covered and she didn't need his help. Then I got her away from him."

"And?" Jaxon pushed.

Gabe took a deep breath. The conversation had gone all wrong. He'd fucked up.

"I told her that she shouldn't talk with a guy like Vincent and that he wasn't right for her. From there on, it got ugly. End of story. I don't want to talk about it."

"You heard about the guy in the woods, and you know none of us plan on leaving her alone in that cottage tonight or any night," Jeb stated.

"Good luck with that. She's on fire right now, and they'll be no negotiating. Trust me, Alana's a hell of a lot tougher than you guys know."

Gabe turned around and began to walk toward the parking lot. He'd screwed up, and she seemed to know that he was pushing her away on purpose yet didn't want to. He needed his buddies. He needed their help and for them to be part of taking care of Alana. The only major problem was that he would be forced to stand by and watch them make love to her when he couldn't share that intimacy with Alana ever again. Not with his scars, the chunk of flesh out of his leg, and his inability to love her fully like they could.

His heart ached something terrible, and a tear nearly fell from his eye.

I love you so goddamn much, Alana. But I can't give you everything you deserve. I can't.

* * * *

Alana was heading toward Gia and Garrett when Gator locked gazes with Gunner, who was standing right beside them.

Gunner knew something was up, and he placed himself in front of Alana and gave Gator the stare down.

"Alana." Gator said her name, and Gunner raised his hand palm forward.

"Slow down, Gator. What's going on? Why is she upset?" Gunner asked in a protective manner.

It both angered Gator because he felt it was his job to protect her and also made him proud. Proud to have such good friends and loyal men like Gunner watching over Alana too.

"Honey, what's wrong?" Gia asked Alana. But instead of seeing tears, or even hearing sniffling or crying, Gator heard Alana practically growl.

"That stupid, hard-headed, delusional Marine. He's pushing me away on purpose because of something stupid. I just know it." Alana said to them.

"Alana, I don't know what happened between you and Gabe back there, but we need to talk." Gator took her hand, pulling her toward him as he pressed closer.

She had tears in her eyes, but her chest was blotchy, probably from getting so angry at Gabe, and her eyes stared at him as she thought of what to say.

When she laid her hand against his chest, he felt his whole world turn upside down. He liked the feel of her feminine, delicate palm against his chest, and he loved how she was petite and he towered over her.

"Alana, you can leave with us right now," Gunner stated firmly.

"I'm taking her home and making sure her place is secure. There's things we're going to discuss," he said to Gunner then looked back down into Alana's eyes.

"Please, Alana, hear me out."

She held his gaze for a few torturous moments, and he thought she would decline and hide behind Gunner, a protective security blanket. Instead, she nodded.

"I'm not angry with you, or even Jaxon, Geno, and Jeb. I'm angry with Gabe."

He wrapped his arm around her waist and held her against his body. He cupped her cheek and stared down into her eyes so she would hopefully see how serious and sincere he was.

"I understand that. I want to talk to you about that, but I also want to make sure that you're safe. I'm going to drive you back to your place and make sure your cottage is secure."

Her eyes widened just as they heard the other voice.

"I'm going too," Geno said as he joined them.

Gia looked at Alana, who turned toward her as she asked, "Are you okay with this?"

Alana didn't answer for a moment, and Gator, who thought he was built of steel, especially around his heart, felt nervous with anticipation.

Alana nodded. "I'll be fine. They really don't have to check the cottage."

Gator glided his hand along her lower back then took her hand and clasped it in his.

"It will make us feel better if we do. Come on. The truck is parked a few rows down."

Alana hugged Gia goodbye then Gunner, Garret, and Wes kissed her cheek and gave Gator and even Geno a warning look. But none of it mattered. Just being with Alana and working out these emotions did.

* * * *

They guided her to a big black truck. Not the same one that the guys had delivered her desk in a couple of weeks ago. Geno had a hand on her lower back, and Gator kept her hand encased in his. She couldn't help it, but it seemed that these men made all her senses work overtime. She was aware of their masculinity, the scents of their colognes, and, of course, the muscles and sex appeal Geno and Gator had.

She'd been touched by only one man before, but here she was getting completely turned on by two right now. However, her mind kept springing back to Gabe and his stupid attitude. What crazy ideas were going through his head? Why did he want to push her away yet seem to want to keep her within arm's reach without touching her or making her his again? It hurt. It really hurt.

The sound of the large truck door opening brought her mind out of the sadness and emotion for a moment. Especially as she reached up to grab the handle at the top of the door to boost her small frame up into the high seat. But then strong arms encased her lower back and under her knees, lifted her up, and placed her into the seat.

She gasped and held on to Geno.

"Scoot on over sexy. Make room for me too."

His brown eyes sparkled, and her inner core pounded. Was that a little cream that leaked from her pussy?

She pulled her bottom lip between her teeth and slid along the seat, even her ass felt sensitive in her tight blue jeans.

She clasped her hands on her lap as Gator, all six feet four of muscle and man in a dark brown shirt bumped into her. She was caught between two huge-ass men, and her whole body erupted with pure lust. She was shocked as he started the engine and the roar of the diesel caused a vibration throughout the vehicle, especially to her more intimate parts. She tried to analyze the effect these men had on her as Gator drove slowly through the parking lot, but her mind couldn't focus, wouldn't focus on anything but the vibrations deep in her cunt and across her nipples that seemed to hum and electrify with the vibrations of the diesel engine.

She gasped and turned to the right as Geno's hand gently covered her knee.

"You're shaking, baby. You're safe with us, don't you know that?" he asked her. His brown eyes, his large presence and masculinity mesmerized her as she nodded like some mute or a teenage girl infatuated with the sexy, older man.

God, and they were older. Maybe ten years, she wasn't sure.

"How old are you guys?" she asked without thinking.

Geno squinted at her as he slowly ran the palm of his hand back and forth on her thigh. With each stroke, his hand moved higher, deeper toward her crotch. She was getting hot, feeling like moving her thighs just slightly farther apart to feel his thick fingers closer to where she seemed to want them.

"Old enough to know what naughty thoughts are going through your head right now, doll."

She was snapped back to realty, feeling caught acting like that teenage girl instead of a grown woman who knew better how to control her own desires. She crossed her legs, forcing his hand out from her inner knee, only for him to clasp both legs and pull her closer to his steely thigh.

As she held his intense gaze, Gator took her hand and placed it on his one thigh as he drove. She was shaking now, and it became obvious how inexperienced she was.

One lover. That's all she'd ever had, and it was Gabe, their roommate and best friend.

She began to feel panicky and tried pulling from their gentle holds.

"Easy, Alana. We just want to hold you, touch you. You're too beautiful to resist," Geno told her.

"I can't do this. I don't know how to react to this," she said as Gator pulled the truck down her street and along the empty dirt roadway that led to Ron's farm and house and then a minute longer before her cottage.

"You should get used to us touching you. It's going to be happening a lot," Geno said, and she gulped.

"About that," she said as Gator parked the truck and turned off that stimulating engine.

Geno raised one eyebrow as she tried to build up the courage to admit she was freaking out and nervous about this. But her silence made him smirk as he opened the door then held a hand out for her to take.

Gator was already out of the truck and coming to the other side. She slid to the edge and gripped the handle at the top of the door, but then Geno placed his hands on her hips and lifted her, making her grab onto his shoulders as he eased her down to her feet. Her breasts rubbed up against his solid chest as she absorbed his cologne and all his manliness at once.

"Baby, you keeping looking at me like that and I'm going to forget all about going slow here."

He reached for her hand and pulled her close as he used his other hand to close the door. The hard sound of metal hitting metal made her jump, and he held her against him, his hand over the upper part of her ass and lower back.

God, he's so big. Even his hands are huge.

Gator's voice interrupted this intense moment, and she was half grateful, even though she thought Geno might kiss her. Instead, she turned, and he guided her by her hips toward the front door.

She fumbled with her key in her purse as Gator walked around to the side of the house and probably the woods to check things out. But that didn't make her nervous at all. She couldn't care less about any strange man in the woods, any Peeping Tom, or anything other than the enormous amount of emotions, desires, and sensations filling her body at this moment. Even as she walked, she felt as though her feet were not touching the floor.

"Alana." Geno said her name, and when she turned to look at him, he had his hands by his sides and appeared too big and tall to fit in her teeny tiny cottage.

She held his gaze.

"Come here," he said, and her heart instantly began to race and pound against her chest.

She stood still, and he raised one of his eyebrows up to her at her lack of response.

Gator opened the front door and walked inside of the house and closed the door behind him.

"It's all clear out there," he said.

"Come. Here. Now," Geno said slowly, with a hint of authority that made her breasts tingle and her pussy ache.

Gator stood still, but her focus was on Geno's deep brown eyes and the seriousness of his command. Everything about these men was military, their intensity, masculinity, and power. It all turned her on entirely too much.

She slowly approached, taking each step with shaky legs and holding this sex god's intense gaze.

He reached out and snagged her around the waist, drawing her tight and hard up against his chest. Geno ran the palm of his hand along her shoulder and under her hair, and then he tilted her head back.

"As I said in the truck, you're too hard to resist."

He leaned down and covered her mouth with his, and she allowed him to take complete control.

* * * *

Geno was caught in a battle with what his dick wanted and what the man wanted right now and in what was the right thing to do for a woman as sweet and perfect as Alana.

But he knew that he wanted her. He wanted to explore every inch of her sexy, curvy, petite body and, of course, her large, full breasts and delicious lips. He pulled her closer as his tongue delved deeper into her mouth in exploration. He couldn't seem to get enough of her taste, the scent of her shampoo, or the feel of femininity and beauty in his arms.

He lifted her higher, cradling her ass with one hand as he kissed her deeply, and she kissed him back.

Their lips parted, and she gasped as he licked along her neck and kissed the skin in the open V of her shirt, his tongue desperate to take a taste of her cleavage and explore lower to her nipple so he could pull and tease her into bliss.

"Geno. Oh God, Geno, you have to stop. We can't—"

Gator moved in from behind her, cupped her cheeks, and then leaned down and kissed her mouth, stopping her from denying this shared attraction.

She reached up with one hand and held Gator's hair and head as he deepened the kiss while her other hand held on to Geno's shoulder. Geno moved her shirt to the side and cupped her breast then licked her skin, circling his tongue, working the material of the bra to the side so he could find her nipple and suckle harder.

She rocked her hips against them, and Geno felt Gator rocking against Alana as their moans filtered through their kisses.

Geno cupped her breast harder and licked across her nipple and pulled when Alana gasped and moaned.

She came. She fucking came in their arms.

His dick instantly hardened and pressed against his jeans, causing him to moan too.

Alana pulled back, her face red, her lips swollen, and her shirt and bra pushed downward, revealing part of her luscious breasts and just how well endowed she was.

"Easy, darling. It's okay. That was bound to happen. You got us both so fucking aroused right now. I'm wondering if your pussy is going to be as sweet as your lips," Gator said, and her eyes widened and she tried to wiggle from Geno's arms. Both men held her in place.

"Whoa, easy, honey," Gator said and pulled her by one of the loops in her jeans closer to him. He cupped her cheek and let his eyes roam over her breasts then smiled softly.

"You pack a hell of a punch. I think all three of us need to slow things down."

She nodded.

"Good girl. Come on now. Let's sit down." Gator took her hand and led her over toward the small couch barely big enough for the three of them to sit.

Back at their ranch they had big couches, plenty of room for sitting and a nice sofa Geno could have spread Alana out on as he tasted that sweet cream he was certain was going to be addicting.

Alana fixed her shirt, crossed her legs, and clasped her hands on her lap, so prim and proper. If it weren't for the fact that they both had made her come in their arms a few moments ago, he would think she was pretending they didn't affect her. But as Gator placed his hand over hers and she slowly looked up into his eyes with desire and hunger, he knew she was just scared and being cautious. There wasn't anything wrong with that, just as long as she didn't deny them what they wanted.

Her.

* * * *

Alana could hardly even focus on the conversation they were having. Not after those kisses, their touches, and how they held her in their arms, suckled her breasts, devoured her moans, and made her come like that. She was initially embarrassed, but now as she sat here feeling the proof of their desires and actions in her panties and against her still swollen pussy, she became more intrigued. Maybe she was just giving into the lust, the attraction because she hadn't had sex in over three years.

She couldn't help but wonder if she had allowed Martin, her friend from Scrantonville, to have sex with her a year ago if she would feel so compelled to give in to these animalistic desires. And they were animalistic. They had to be. Because with Geno and Gator kissing her, and touching her, she wanted to do nothing more then rip their clothes off, suckle their skin, and taste their cocks as they fucked her long and hard. She felt almost desperate to come and to feel that sensation she hadn't felt since Gabe.

This was such a screwed-up situation. They were Gabe's brothers in arms, his military buddies, his best friends and roommates, and they wanted her. Why couldn't Gabe want her too?

She felt the tear in her eyes and then Gator's hand caress her cheek.

"Talk to us. We're the only ones saying how we're feeling and what we think will work here. Come on, Alana. This isn't something we're all forcing on you. The attraction is real, the feelings mutual," Gator told her.

"I know that. I do," she whispered with her hands clasped on her lap as she wrung them together. Her heart was beating fast, and she felt embarrassed to admit her desires and her lack of sexual experience in so many years.

"I don't know if this is right, or if I'm just desperate."

"Desperate? What do you mean?" Geno asked her.

She eased up off the couch, and both men sat there staring at her filling up her small gray sofa with their huge bodies.

"Desperate for sex, to come, to orgasm, and feel alive and whole again. God, why are you making me say this? I don't want to hurt anyone's feelings, yet I feel like I would be the only one suffering here."

"What are you saying? Do you think this is just lust?" Geno asked her.

"It has to be. Look at you guys. You're sexy, have big muscles, and you're Marines. I'm not stupid. You're women's fantasies come true, and I haven't had sex in over three years," she blurted out.

Their eyes widened, and she covered her face with her hands and felt as though she wanted to cry, but also laugh.

Gator stood up and gently pulled her hands from her face.

"That's not something to be embarrassed about. I'm sure there were opportunities, although I don't want to hear about them."

"Me either," Geno grunted as he moved closer.

"I didn't mean to blurt that out. You probably think I'm immature. But I chose not to have sex. Nothing, no one made me feel like giving in. Especially as I kept hoping, praying, that Gabe was alive." Her chest tightened, and she hoped she wasn't upsetting them by admitting that.

"Honey, we understand all that. Perhaps knowing that he's alive and well, and that he wants us all to be together is making it easier for you to give in? Your body knows what it wants. Hell, what is your heart telling you?" Geno asked.

"I don't know. It's been broken for so long," she admitted.

Gator cupped her cheek.

"I think that you're overthinking everything. You need to slow down and just go with it. Follow your gut, and you'll see that we're all good men who care for you already. This is what we wanted to talk to you about. We want to get to know you better. We want to take care of you. We can't do that if you close up and fight your emotions and feelings because of the past and because of Gabe."

"But, Gator, he's your roommate and your friend. How can we give this relationship a try when all I keep thinking about is Gabe and why he can't love me the way I've always loved him? It hurt so badly to believe that he died or was missing in action. He's the only man I ever loved and that I ever let make love to me. I know you guys are older and have probably had your share of women, but I need that connection, that bond. I can't just have sex."

"No one is asking you to," Geno said.

"What are you asking of me then?"

"To give this relationship, a ménage relationship with five men, a try," Gator told her.

"Five? But there's only four of you."

"Right now there are only four of us, but mark my words, Alana, Gabe is going to be part of this relationship sooner or later. You mean just as much to him as he does to you. He's just going through this battle within himself right now and nothing has seemed to penetrate that shield he put up," Gator said.

"Until you. From the moment he saw you at the estate sale, we all saw a change in him. He just needs to work through his problems. But in the meantime, we all get to work on getting to know one another and seeing where this mutual attraction brings us. So will you give it a try?" Geno asked.

She swallowed hard and hoped that Gabe would come around and not be angry that she was getting romantically involved with his friends.

"I'll try Geno. I'll try."

"Good. Now let's work on perfecting the three-way kiss we were working on before. I liked that. A lot," Geno said and raised both eyebrows up and down.

She felt her cheeks blush as she smiled, and Gator gave Geno a light shove to his shoulder as he shook his head at him, as if Geno was being a moron.

Her heart felt lighter, and her spirit lifted at the possibilities. She was going to try a ménage relationship, and even these men wanted Gabe to eventually be part of it. A new hope arose inside of her, a new fight within to make Gabe realize he could be a part of this and a part of her again too. Time would tell, and hopefully this wouldn't do the opposite and tear them further apart. Then she would more than likely have to leave Tranquility and a life that had meant nothing without Gabe in it.

Chapter 3

He watched her from afar as he filtered through the clothing rack pretending to locate a blue button-down shirt. He would need one for the night he planned. It was a little distraction, a gift to himself for being so patient as he waited for Alana. God, just saying her name made his heart race and his dick harden. He adjusted his glasses, a little disguise to make him appear timid, kind of shy, and approachable. Women tended to feel more comfortable with a man who was nerdy and approachable than one who sported all his muscles.

Neil hid his muscles and his rock-hard abs well beneath the confines of bulky clothing. He trained excessively. He loved the rush of a good workout. To train until exhaustion hit him. To wake up chilled to the bone from a cold sweat on the basement floor made him feel as though he'd achieved something and he was an animal.

No man was capable of bringing him down. None ever were. Not in the service, not in the police department, and not in the damn hospital he was forced to live in over two years ago.

He nearly shivered from the memory. The howling and crying of other patients at night. Being treated like some low-life animal instead of a human being who needed compassion and care. No, instead they mocked him. Especially that one nurse. The stupid, ugly bitch. She mocked him. Turned him down when he asked her out and then sent her flowers at her home once he was released.

She'd suffered the consequences for denying his advances. And just like the others, she was gone forever, and no one would ever find them.

"Excuse me, can I help you?" He heard the deeper, older voice of the owner of the store, Mrs. Hamlet.

He was annoyed. He wanted Alana to help him.

"I'm just looking, but thank you."

"You seem like you are looking for something specific. Perhaps I could direct you to where you might find it?" she asked.

"Is Alana here? She helped me the last time and knew exactly what I needed."

The older woman gave him a peculiar expression, and he widened one eye at the old bitch who finally seemed to get the hint that he meant business. Yeah, once a soldier of power, always a soldier of power.

"Let me see if she's available. I think she's going on her lunch break," Mrs. Hamlet said, and as she turned, Alana was heading toward them.

"Mrs. Hamlet, I'm going to go out to grab some lunch with some friends for my break. Can I get you anything while I'm out?"

"That's okay. My husband will be bringing along some things shortly. Allison and Monique are still sorting the new shipment, right?"

"Oh yes, they are. If you need me to stay a little longer I can tell my friends to go ahead without me."

"No, don't be silly. I'll get Monique to come out front."

"Okay, I'll see you in thirty minutes." Alana said then walked out.

He watched Alana, looking so lovely and sweet in her knee-length black skirt that hugged her sexy figure and the pale green blouse that matched her eyes. It wasn't low cut either from what he could see from this distance, but he could still tell that she was well endowed. His mouth watered at thoughts of how he would strip her from those clothes when the time was right. She wore low heels, and her legs were sexy too, just like the rest of her. His attention went to the chiming of the bells against the main door as Mrs. Hamlet asked him if she could help him again, but he ignored her. His eyes locked onto the two big men who entered the store and greeted Alana with kisses to her cheek.

Neil gripped the hanger, hearing the crack as Alana walked out with two men.

She's mine, you fuckers. You can't have her.

Mrs. Hamlet gasped as the hanger snapped. He dropped it to the floor and walked away, cursing under his breath.

* * * *

"Damn, woman, you are a sight," Jaxon told Alana when he and Jeb met her at the clothing store. She shyly looked down, and Jaxon placed his finger under her chin, tilted it up toward him, and kissed her.

It was a short kiss, but he hoped tonight they would all have some deeper, longer kisses with her.

"Hey, beautiful. What are you in the mood for?" Jeb asked as he gently pushed a stray hair from her cheek then leaned down and kissed her next.

She fanned herself and started walking.

"My God, the two of you are lethal. I don't care. You guys choose. I only have thirty minutes."

"Well then, let's hurry, but tonight, you're coming to our place, and we're cooking for you."

"Really?" she asked as if she didn't believe they would, or perhaps she didn't believe they were capable.

"We're all really good at cooking, and tonight, Gabe, Geno, and Gator are in charge of dinner."

Alana stared at him but then looked away. He realized that every time they mentioned Gabe she reacted. Sadness showed in her eyes, but he was hoping the more they did it, the more accustomed she would get to thinking of them as one team, one group of men interested in making her their woman.

Jeb took her hand, and Jaxon placed his at her lower back as they headed around the corner to a small little deli and café. Tranquility was small and slowly growing as more people moved there. He remembered when they'd arrived. Five lost souls, soldiers in search of putting the past behind them and moving on to a calmer, safer lifestyle. They had given so much of themselves to the Marine Corps, though some had given the ultimate sacrifice.

That thought made him think about Gabe. He was a mess when they arrived, and the locals, the ones in charge of running this town and allowing people to move in, had their concerns. He was violent, filled to the gills with anger and hatred for everyone. He wanted to die, yet he wouldn't take his own life. That would be a disgrace to the Corps and to his team, his brothers in arms.

Jaxon swallowed the small lump of emotion in his throat. This woman, this petite, sweet, gorgeous, young woman, could make a difference in all their lives, and especially in Gabe's.

"Let's take that small table over there in the corner by the window," Jeb suggested as they headed that way.

They waved or smiled at a few patrons in the place. Locals who worked in town and were on lunch break just like Alana. The men looked at her, their eyes gazing over her figure and her long, tan legs. As Jeb released her to sit, Jaxon gripped her hips and pressed against her back, holding her in place before she sat. He leaned forward and kissed her neck, making her gasp softly then turn slightly toward him.

"Have I told you how much I like your outfit, especially this skirt?" he asked.

She looked at him peculiarly, as if she were on to his possessive tactics of staking a public claim.

"It's just a plain black skirt."

He shook his head. "Not on you. It shows your shapely figure and long sexy thighs, and my favorite part is how accessible it is." He ran a hand along the hem as if he would raise it up right here in the deli, and she slapped his hand away and turned to sit.

"Jaxon," she reprimanded and took the seat next to Jeb, who looked hungry and aroused.

He leaned closer to her. "Sure you have to go back to work today? Jaxon and I would love to find out what you're hiding under that skirt."

"Stop it, Jeb, you're making a scene," she reprimanded, lowering her head, blushing. It was obvious by her red cheeks she was embarrassed by the attention.

Both of them chuckled then lifted up the specials menu.

"What do you feel like having?" Jaxon asked.

"Alana," Jeb teased.

Jaxon chuckled as his buddy played along, obviously feeling the same things he was feeling. Alana released an annoyed sigh.

"If you're going to do this to me, then I won't be having lunch with either of you again."

Jaxon widened his eyes as he took her hand and held it.

"Now, darling, don't be making any threats. You behave, or there'll be trouble." He winked at her.

"What kind of—"

She gulped, and her cheeks turned a brighter shade of pink.

She might be a bit inexperienced, but she got the hint of his meaning.

She cleared her throat.

"I think I'll just have the chicken salad sandwich."

Jeb smiled. "I'll go place the order. Jaxon, what about you?"

Jaxon ordered an Italian combo and an iced tea and then watched Jeb walk up to the counter to place the order.

He turned toward Alana, and she was watching Jeb too. In fact, she looked to be checking out his ass.

* * * *

Alana felt as though her body was going to snap. It was taking all the self-control she could muster not to tell Jeb and Jaxon that she wanted them to kiss her, touch her, and just hold her in their big, strong arms. But she couldn't be so brazen. She was feeling uneasy and overwhelmed. They were both so big and handsome. Jaxon with his striking blue eyes, blond hair, and commanding demeanor was intimidating. Jeb's deep brown eyes and dark hair made him seem so hard-core, mysterious, and powerful.

All four of the men were to die for. Geno with his brown hair and light brown eyes had the softer, more approachable personality, yet he seemed meticulous, orderly, and in charge. Then there was Gator. God, she'd thought of Gator just this morning when she was showering. He was the tallest of the men, with jet-black hair, military styled, and dark blue eyes that bored right through to her soul. He stood at six feet four inches, and she was a shrimp when he was nearby. It made her feel protected, shielded by anything bad or evil, and that, of course, made her aroused and downright horny.

She took a deep breath and released it as Jaxon watched her. These were Marines. Capable, hard, never-give-up-or-give-in Marines. Lordy was she in a heap of trouble.

"So how is work going today?" he asked her.

"Fine so far. They got in a new shipment of fall clothing, so we're trying to rearrange the racks. You know, place things on the discount or sale racks and then set up the new displays. We have to re-tag all the old items and then place new tags on the new items so they ring up properly at the front register. It's busy work, so it makes the time go by."

"Which do you like better, the boutique or working at Casper's?"

"Well, besides clothing there are other popular items sold in the boutique so it keeps me busy. I like working at Casper's because it's harder work physically. I'm constantly moving around, and there are so many people to meet."

He looked a little angry for a flash of a second, and she squinted at him.

"Jaxon, what's wrong?" she asked.

He licked his lower lip as if he were processing his thoughts before he responded to her.

"There are a lot of guys who hang out there, especially at the bar."

"And your point is what?"

He leaned closer and held her gaze with a firm expression.

"They have their eyes on you. Looking your body over, trying to flirt and take an opportunity to touch you. I don't like it, okay? It pisses me off." He nearly spat the last words.

He was jealous, and the thought did something to her. She reacted. She reached up and placed her palm against his chin. She held his gaze.

"Don't be jealous. It's just a job to help me make ends meet. Those guys don't mean anything, but you, Jeb, Geno, and Gator do. I like you guys, so remember that, please."

He looked at her lips and began to move forward, but she beat him to it and kissed him softly on the lips.

She loved how his masculine, gruff skin felt against her palm. He was sexy and manly and everything her body, her heart, and soul found appealing.

"Here we go." Jeb returned, carrying a tray of food. She released Jaxon and smiled at Jeb.

"Thank you, Jeb."

"You can thank me with a kiss like you just gave Jaxon," he teased her as he leaned closer.

She placed her palm against his cheek and smiled right before she kissed him softly on the lips.

"Now that's what I'm talking about."

They chuckled and then began to sort out the food and eat lunch together in the small deli and café. Alana felt comfortable and actually happy, for the first time in quite a while, and that she needed time to process.

* * * *

Gunner McCallister stood in the office of the local police station in Salvation. As a Texas Ranger and a resident of Salvation, he worked a lot of the cases nearby and in the town. Over the last several years, he'd noticed the increase in population as well as the increase in criminal activity. For the most part, their law enforcement agencies, in a cooperative effort, had been staying on top of things. However, as he stood there with Jim and Teddy, two detectives, he couldn't help shake the funny feeling he had about this latest murder.

"So where are you two in the investigation?" he asked them.

"The victim was alone, no family, and had just moved into Salvation a few months ago. By the intensity of the violence committed upon her, we believe that the killer knew her, perhaps intimately," Jim said.

Gunner squinted his eyes and felt the anger begin to boil within him.

"Are you thinking about an ex-boyfriend or lover?" he asked.

"Could be. Duke, Shane, and Gerry are working on that theory now. So far they've found out she came from Houston, had told a few friends that she felt like someone was watching her, and then, within a few weeks, she packed up her things and left town," Teddy explained.

"I wonder if she knew who had been watching her. But why she didn't report him? We need to find that guy. I think I'll take a ride into Houston and see what I can dig up. She had to confide in someone. She was twenty-one years old, working at a local restaurant as a waitress, and taking college classes. There has to be more to this."

"We'll keep digging on our end and hopefully come up with something more concrete or a clue. Her family is distraught, and they're demanding that her killer be found," Teddy added.

"And rightfully so. We'll find the one responsible. I'll keep in touch."

Gunner headed out of the office then out of the building to his car. He couldn't help but think about Gia and the two men who'd tried to forcefully take her, never mind that dick Jeffrey who'd attacked her. Men who went after women like that needed to be locked up and beaten. Someone had hurt this young woman, Samantha, very badly before they left her to die. The crime scene was horrific and definitely personal. He was out there, and Gunner would do what he could to find this guy and to bring justice to Samantha's family.

Chapter 4

Alana sat on the living room floor, sweaty and tired from the workout video she did. She had wanted to go for a run but felt she didn't have enough time to do so. As she gathered some energy, she got up and headed to the bathroom. She needed a shower and wanted to look good for tonight.

As she let the water cascade over her body, she thought about the way the men made her feel. She wondered if she could allow Jaxon, Geno, Gator, and Jeb touch her when in the past any other man than Gabe made her panic and push them away. What was it about these Marines that had her considering having sex again?

Could it be how much they reminded her of Gabe or the simple fact they were his room mates and best friends so they represented safety? It seemed screwed up to allow those type of feelings make her give her body so freely.

But that thought didn't sit right either. This confusion, the hunger for them was what led her to do the damn workout video. She was trying to clear her head and work out this need in her body. But instead her mind was consumed with getting involved in a ménage with four men and having sex again after three years of nothing.

She stepped out of the shower and dried off.

Alana put on some facial cream and then some special body lotion. She reapplied a little makeup. Not much, just some lip gloss and eye shadow. She sprayed her perfume and even made sure she'd shaved and was smooth in all the right places. That got her pausing and staring at herself in her mirror.

Her breasts looked fuller, her cheeks had a light blush to them, and she appeared happy. How could that be? How could meeting Gabe's four best friends and roommates make her feel alive again? She swallowed the lump of emotion and battled for the umpteenth time over how she could consider getting intimately involved with four men, maybe five if Gabe got his head out of his ass.

She covered her mouth and gasped at her own thoughts. Holy shit, she was considering this. Hell, she was contemplating how it would play out and how intense and overwhelming sex could be for someone like her.

She felt the tears hit her eyes. She was inexperienced, small, and susceptible to their masculinity and charms. They were all big all over from muscles to personalities. She was shy, soft-spoken, not delicate in a way that she was fearful, weak, or timid, but more reserved. Could she handle four men? Could she handle any man other than Gabe touching her, fucking her?

She felt her cheeks warm and her pussy spasm, and she thought of them. All four sexy, eye candy Marines that wanted little ol' her.

She stared at her body in the mirror. Her bra barely covered her full, large breasts. The belly ring she wore was sexy and youthful against her tight abs she worked so hard to maintain. Exercise had helped her deal with her emotions and the loss of Gabe. She worked out sometimes to exhaustion so her mind would stop thinking of him and missing him.

She ran her hand along her panties, tiny, sexy, black, and lacy. Would Jaxon like them? Would Geno be aroused by the piercing? Would Gator take his time making love to her, or would he lift her up and sink his cock in deep and fuck her hard against the wall? She closed her eyes and nearly moaned.

Jeb would surely take his time. He had big hands, capable hands that would take from her, make her beg to come.

Her eyes popped open, and she smirked. "You're more than ready for this. You want them, and they want you. So what that Gabe is there? If he wants you still, then he will join them. Just relax and let go. If it falls apart, and things get all fucked up then at least you enjoyed the ride and the experience."

Her heart hammered in her chest. She was never so brazen and calm when it came to sex or giving up her heart to someone. How the hell was she going to handle these men and have enough love to give each of them? What if they stopped caring? Would it hurt like Gabe not loving her anymore does? This was a greater risk than maybe she really understood. Perhaps letting go and lowering her guard wasn't the answer. Maybe protecting her heart was the only logical thing to do?

* * * *

Gabe was sautéing the vegetables as Geno made the chicken saltimbocca. He was adding the prosciutto and the sage and preparing the pan for the chicken.

Gabe couldn't believe he was doing this. His team was all showered, shaved, and ready to seduce Alana. And that was exactly what they were going to do. They wanted her. They were all attracted to her and saw her for the perfect woman she was. Smart, beautiful, a good head on her shoulders, and a body that aroused each of them, including himself. His mind focused on the ache in his leg, a constant reminder of his inability to satisfy her the way a perfect man could. It was a constant, throbbing pain that nothing made subside. Thinking of Alana, wanting her, needing her made the pain increase and his mind set him straight. He couldn't have her. Not fully, not alone, not with this injury and with the scars on his soul.

"Pass the salt," Geno said to him, and he nearly tossed the little glass shaker at him.

"Yo, what's up with you? You're going to burn the veggies," Geno reprimanded.

He took the spatula from Gabe and moved the vegetables around in the large frying pan. They had a commercial stove and oven. They all enjoyed cooking but not entertaining. They never entertained except for a few football games with pizza and beers.

"Okay, what do you guys need help with?" Jaxon asked as he entered the room. "Jeb went to pick up Alana."

Gabe looked him over. His commander, the leader of their team, one of his best friends, his brother, was dressed to kill. He wore a burgundy button-down shirt, with the first two buttons undone, dark black dress pants, black cowboy boots, as well as cologne. He was also clean-shaven and looking ready to get laid.

Gabe's teeth clenched, and his heart pounded. But he wasn't jealous. He was envious. Why couldn't he appear perfect, unscathed by the demons of war, violence, and near-death? Why couldn't he let go of the feelings of inadequacy and just embrace the one woman, the one person who completed him and made everything okay?

Because he wasn't that big of a dick. Alana deserved men like Jaxon, Geno, Gator, and Jeb, who could put the war, the scars, and their pasts behind them and move on.

"Gabe? Gabe, what the fuck are you staring at?" Jaxon asked, interrupting his thoughts.

"You look like you're going to a fucking club," Gabe snapped at him.

Geno chuckled.

"Jealous?" Geno teased.

"Fuck no. Jealous of that old guy? I don't think so," Gabe replied with an angry attitude.

"Hey, I don't think I look bad. This is my best fucking dress shirt." Jaxon fixed the collar and ran his hand along the waistband to make sure it was tucked in neatly. It was so tight and tucked in it looked like his military uniform. Once a Marine, always a Marine.

"That's because everything else you own is either military green, black, or some shade of blue. It looks good. I was just fucking with ya," Gabe told him, and Jaxon held his gaze and gave a small smirk.

"That's what you're wearing?"

What?" Gabe asked, putting down the spatula and turning off the burner. Gabe fixed the navy blue dress shirt and adjusted the waist on his black dress pants.

"Nothing's wrong with it. You never get dressed up. You're always in camo pants and T-shirts."

"Yeah well, we never have company. Alana is a lady, so remember that," Gabe barked and turned around. He could hear them chuckle low. But then he heard the door open and a slow whistle fill the room.

Gator was staring at something and not moving an inch.

"What's up?" Geno asked as he placed the last piece of chicken onto the serving platter.

"She's here, and holy fuck she looks incredible," Gator whispered.

Jeb opened the front door, and Gator headed that way.

Gabe closed his eyes and willed himself to remain calm and just let this happen. It was best for Alana. His team would protect her, care for her, and perhaps love her the way he wasn't capable of.

"Damn, baby, you are a sight," he heard Gator say, and then Gabe turned around to take a look for himself, and he nearly lost his ability to stand.

* * * *

Gator pulled Alana into his arms and hugged her to him. He ran his hand along her ass and over the tight beige skirt she wore. In high heels, she still had to stand up on tiptoes to kiss him, and he loved that about her. She was petite, feminine, and she smelled edible.

He sniffed her hair and then slowly let her lower after she pressed her lips gently to his.

His eyes roamed over the cleavage of her blouse, low cut, sexy, and a pale pink. She was a knockout.

"I missed you," he told her.

"That's real sweet, Gator. I missed you too. What smells so good in here?" she asked as he released her, only for Geno to pull her into his arms and kiss her next.

"Chicken saltimbocca with sautéed vegetables, thanks to Gabe, and some roasted red potatoes, thanks to Gator," Geno told her as he pressed his hands over her waist and absorbed her beauty.

Gator watched her lay her hands gently on Geno's arms and smile. "I'm impressed."

"Wait until you taste it. But how about a drink first?" Gator asked.

Geno released her, and Jaxon was there to take her hand and bring it to his lips. He kissed her knuckles, and she smiled. "Sure. What do you have?"

"A glass of wine good?" Jaxon asked her.

"Perfect."

He released her hand, and Gabe stood there staring at her. It was an intense moment, and Gator wondered what would happen as the others stood there watching. Alana shocked them when she stepped closer and held out her hand to shake Gabe's.

"Nice to see you, Gabe. I see you're still a whiz in the kitchen."

Gabe looked at her hand and then at her body.

"And you're still as beautiful as ever."

The air was so thick you could cut a knife through it, and Gabe moved to the side, avoiding any physical contact with her whatsoever. But Gator wasn't stupid. Alana got to Gabe just like the rest of them. She would be theirs. He would bet his life on that.

* * * *

Alana was relieved when Jaxon handed her a glass of wine. She wondered if she could even hold the glass she was shaking so hard. To see Gabe, to get that reaction from him, but for him not to touch her made her irate. But she got to him. She could see it in his eyes, his body language, and that was a plus as far as making progress went.

"Thank you, Jaxon. What are you guys having?" She took a sip and turned toward the others.

They were all standing there looking her over as though she was the meal instead of the fancy chicken dish. Her pussy clenched, and she took several sips of liquid courage until Jeb placed his hand at her lower back.

"We're having beer. Jaxon and Gabe are the ones who like wine. How about we go sit in the living room?" Jeb suggested.

"Your home is so big. Could I get a tour? Do we have enough time before dinner?"

Jeb smiled at her.

"Of course. Bring your wine," he said, and she followed him out of the kitchen with Jaxon, Gator, and Geno behind them. Gabe remained behind.

As they showed her their home, she realized pretty quickly that they maintained their military structure and cleanliness. Everything had a place, an order in every room. The decorations were scarce, and the furnishings perfect, but not lived in. Their bedrooms were a different story, starting with Jeb's.

"This is nice, Jeb. I guess you're into world history?" She ran her hands along the many historical books on war and on weapons. He had some models of intricate weaponry on his desk shelf and a few paintings on the walls of Marine Corps history.

His bed was big with a thick hunter-green comforter and burgundy pillows, but it was devoid of any decorative pillows or even a blanket.

She was looking at the few personal items on the shelf, trying to get an understanding of Jeb, when he wrapped an arm around her waist and pulled her close. She set her wine glass down so it wouldn't spill, and he kissed along her neck.

"You smell so good baby," he whispered.

His lips seared her skin, and she turned in his arms and kissed him back. Then someone cleared their throat, reminding them that they weren't alone. They parted, and Jaxon handed her the glass of wine, giving a stern expression to Jeb before they headed out of the room and into Gator's room.

Apparently he was into strong men contests, weight lifting, and music. A saxophone lay on a stand in the corner next to another containing music sheets. There was even a small amplifier on the floor.

"Gator, you play the saxophone?" she asked him.

He nodded but looked a little worried that she wouldn't like that.

She touched his arm and smiled.

"That is so cool. Can you play something?"

"Right now?" he asked.

"If the others don't mind." She looked at Jeb, Jaxon, and Geno.

"Go ahead, big guy, impress the woman," Geno added and crossed his arms in front of his chest.

Alana smiled as Gator sat down and began to play some sexy, slow jazz song.

She was swaying to the sound, smiling wide and truly impressed when Geno took her hand, handed the wine glass to Jaxon, and began to dance slowly with her in Gator's bedroom. The sound of the jazz music and the feel of Geno's hands holding her, caressing her was arousing to say the least.

With Jeb and Jaxon watching, she became even more aroused, and then Geno ran the palm of his hand along her ass then to her waist before cupping her breast.

She gasped, and he kissed her, catching her moan and swinging their hips to the music.

It was erotic and sexy, and then she felt the second set of hands on her hips from behind, and a thick, hard cock pressed against the seam of her ass.

Geno released her lips but continued to suckle her skin along her neck. Jaxon ran his hands along her hips and her thighs then toward the front of her skirt and under the material.

"Open for me, baby. Let me feel how turned on you are," Jaxon whispered.

She did exactly what he asked without preamble or fear. She wanted their touch. She craved the power of the desire they brought out in her. Geno helped her part her thighs by pressing hers wider with his leg. The moment she felt Jaxon's hands against her skin and along her groin, she panicked and tightened.

"Easy, baby. It's us. We want to pleasure you and make you feel comfortable with all of us," Jaxon told her then kissed her neck.

Her head rolled back, and Geno licked along her cleavage. She grabbed his head and held it as he pressed her blouse then bra to the side and twirled his tongue along the inside of her bra and against her nipple.

Then she felt the thick, warm fingers brush across her silk panties.

"Someone is wearing some very sexy panties." Jaxon's fingers explored farther, to the crease of her ass. She began to breathe more rapidly.

"Thong. She's wearing a thong," Jaxon whispered then maneuvered his finger underneath the material and right against her pussy lips.

"Fuck that's hot. I knew it," Gator said, making her horny just thinking that Gator and the others might have been fantasizing about her.

"Oh God." She moaned and felt Geno undoing the buttons to her blouse. She grabbed his hands.

"Geno."

"Shh, baby, just exploring a little. We'll only go as far as you're ready for. You're so gorgeous. Too difficult to resist."

"Too difficult to not take a taste of or sample," Jaxon added then pressed a digit up into her pussy.

Alana moaned and moved forward, only for Jaxon to hold her back with one arm wrapped around her midsection. In front of her, Geno unclipped her bra, revealing her large breasts to their view. She panted and pressed her chest outward as Geno licked along one breast and Gator joined in cupping the other.

"Oh God, this is too much," she said, and Jeb cupped her cheeks and stared down into her eyes with a very serious, determined, expression.

"This is right. You're right for us, and we're right for you."

He kissed her as Jaxon thrust fingers in and out of her cunt so fast, so deep she began to rock her hips, and finally, she exploded. Right there in front of four men she lusted over, she came.

Her entire body felt weak from this erotic episode, but strong arms embraced her, holding her up. Jeb caressed her cheeks as Jaxon removed his fingers and fixed her panties and skirt. Gator and Geno kissed her lips one after the next as she fixed her bra and then her blouse.

"Dinner is more than ready."

Alana gasped and turned toward the doorway. There stood Gabe, leaning on his cane, his eyes hooded and dark and his expression as clear as day. He was aroused and hungry, but he turned and walked away.

* * * *

"What the fuck," Gabe grunted at Jaxon as he met him in the hallway after Alana and the others headed downstairs to the kitchen.

"What?" Jaxon asked him with his arms crossed in front of his chest.

Gabe raised his voice. "She's here for ten fucking minutes and you guys were about to strip her naked and fuck her against the fucking wall in Gator's room? What the fuck?"

"You should have joined us. She's really sweet," Jaxon said and let his fingers pass over his nose as if he were inhaling her scent on his fingers.

Gabe grabbed him and shoved him against the wall.

"She's a lady, and she's too inexperienced and fragile to just fuck and use," Gabe grunted.

"You're so worried about how we're handling this attraction then maybe you should step in and join us. Maybe show us what gets Alana all hot and ready for cock."

Gabe felt as if his head were about to explode, but then he saw that look in his commander's eyes. He was challenging him, doing this on purpose so he would react, and that was exactly what he'd done.

"Fuck it. If she wants to fuck you guys tonight, then so be it." He started to walk away even though he didn't want to. He didn't want to think about them touching her and having her without him present. How fucked up was that? He wanted to be there and watch them take her one after the next or even together.

Jaxon grabbed his upper arm and stopped him.

"You fucking love her. You want her just as much as we do. So get your head out of your ass and take what's yours. We can all make her happy, Gabe. We can all claim her as our woman so no other men can ever touch her or have her but us. We can help you through whatever it is that's holding you back. Just fucking go for it, will ya?" He released Gabe's arm with a hard shove and headed back to the kitchen.

Gabe ran his fingers through his hair and banged his fist against the wall.

Jaxon was right. He wanted Alana, too, and he might not be able to stop himself from participating. But come tomorrow, he might just push her away again for her own good.

* * * *

Alana listened as the men talked about how much of a hardass Jaxon was as their commander. She couldn't help but smile and take in the man's body as he ate his dinner or took a drink from his wine glass, ignoring their teasing. The muscles in his neck flexed, and he seemed to relax a little with his sleeves rolled up and his muscles bulging.

He was definitely still their leader in a lot of ways. A hand gesture, an expression, a look in his eyes and the others responded without thought, just instinctually.

It made her gain a greater respect for their service as Marines, as well as giving her a great respect for Jaxon. He was a commander like her father had been.

"I have a lot of respect for you, Jaxon, as I'm certain your men here do. It takes a special man to remain in charge and calm during the heated missions you guys just described," Alana told him, and he held her gaze from across the table. He almost looked embarrassed.

"Don't give him so many kudos, Alana. There were times he wasn't so calm and collected," Geno teased.

"Like when?" Jaxon asked.

"Ah, let's see, that night we jumped from the chopper and the new troop fucked up the location. We landed in a swamp full of shit and overflow from the small shit town's sewage system. So not state-of-the-art," Geno told them.

"Ah fuck, I remember that. I smelled like, well, bad for days," Gator said, trying to not curse so much in front of her.

"That's terrible," she said, and they all gave their thoughts of on their memories of that day.

"Yeah, he wasn't so pleasant, let me tell ya," Jeb added about Jaxon.

"Well, from what you describe, that sounds understandable. How could anyone keep calm when a troop screws up like that and makes you fall into a swamp of—"

"Shit," Jaxon said, and they all chuckled.

Alana looked at him and smiled.

"It's not easy being in charge of a troop of men and women. Their lives depend on you and your judgments, your decisions and orders. I'm sure people aren't lining up to be commanders in the Marine Corps."

"You sound like you know what it's like," Jaxon said then took a sip of wine and held her gaze.

She glanced at the others, and they were all watching her, listening to her, except for Gabe. He was trying so hard to ignore her.

"Well, I kind of know first-hand what it's like. My dad was a commander in the Old Breed for most of my childhood and teenage years."

"The first Marine Division? He's one of us?" Gator asked, sitting forward in his seat.

"*Was* one of you. He died five years ago," she told them and lowered her eyes to her lap.

"I'm so sorry, Alana. Was it during active duty?" Geno asked her.

She shook her head. "A drunk driver and his friends smashed into my parents' truck on the highway leading into Scrantonville. They were on their way home from my dad's friend's fiftieth birthday dinner. I was told they died instantly." She glanced over at Gabe.

"The driver was three times over the blood alcohol limit. He shouldn't even have been conscious, never mind driving," Gabe added, and she looked up at him and held his gaze. He'd been there for her during that time. He left for the Corps a year later.

"That's just insane," Gator said and squeezed her shoulder. She smiled at him.

"My dad was a tough man, a true Marine. He was proud of this country and of his service. My mom loved him so much too. It was hard on her, and on me, but we survived those times when he was away. My mom even got angry sometimes, I think because she was lonely, but then he would return from a mission or a tour and she was all happy and smiling again. I know he lived a full life. I just wish I could have had more time with him as a civilian," she confessed.

"Did you have any other family around? You know people to help you? You had to be about eighteen," Jeb asked her.

"I had friends and the townspeople. I had Gabe and his family." She glanced up at him. The others did too, and they looked surprised.

"Scrantonville was like that. If anyone needed anything or someone was in trouble, down and out, the people in town came together in support of one another," she told them but held Gabe's gaze.

"What did you do in Scrantonville when you lived there?" Geno asked.

"I worked for a law office and also the local restaurant and bar during the holidays and weekends."

"So you lived all alone?" Jeb asked her.

"Yes. I got used to it, especially once Gabe left. I had my job and, of course, the fundraisers. Like the one Gabe's parents and the locals in town started when he didn't return from his tours." Alana shot a look at Gabe. He sat forward.

"What?"

"Oh, yeah, in an attempt to not let your sacrifice to our country be forgotten, your parents and I, along with the others in town who loved you and thought so much of you, started a scholarship organization. A fundraising program to assist returning soldiers with finding jobs and having their own homes and any extra support they might need as they transitioned into civilian life. Every year we would meet for a memorial in honor of your life and your sacrifice. Loads of people came. People I never had even seen or met before. It's helped a lot of people."

He slammed his fist down on the table and stood up. "I never asked for that. I never expected anything from anyone," he shouted.

Alana held his gaze. "Well, people thought a lot of you, Gabe. They respected you and your sacrifice. They hoped that you would return and set roots there or nearby. Your parents hoped so too."

"They shouldn't have done that. I'm not important enough for something like that. Why couldn't they just leave it alone and let me be dead to them so I can deal with this alone?" he asked in anger.

She stood up and placed her hands on the table as she leaned forward and held his gaze.

"Because, you stupid bastard, we all loved you with all our hearts, and still do. But you're so self absorbed in your goddamn injury, your scars, or whatever has you limping around feeling sorry for yourself that you couldn't face the best power, the greatest medicine for anything you have. It's called love, you moron. You have an entire town filled with it, and instead of taking advantage, you wuss out and pretend to be dead. I cried my eyes out every goddamn night over you, Gabe. I prayed for your safe return. I would have given my life for yours. I asked God to take me and bring you back." She slammed her hand down and jumped up to walk away.

She heard the banging against the table, chairs scraped against the hardwood floors, and as she turned, she saw Gabe heading toward her. He paused just a few feet in front of her. The others took protective positions around them.

"Gabe?" Jaxon whispered his name, and Gabe shook his head.

She could see the tears in Gabe's eyes and the full force of the anger she'd brought out in him as she stared up into his eyes.

"You deserve better than me and what I can give you."

"Bullshit!" she exclaimed.

His eyes widened.

"I'm not like your father, Alana. He went through all those years kicking ass, gaining medal after medal, and came home to you and your mom whole and perfect. I'm not whole, and I'm not perfect."

"You were perfect for me. I would have taken you back, no matter what. And for the record, my dad wasn't perfect. My dad suffered every damn night when he would wake up in a cold sweat, sometimes straddling my mom, lost in the war in his head. She was there to comfort him and calm him down and to let him know that he was safe and okay. He accepted that. I would have done that for you because, like my mother loved my father, with her heart and soul, I loved you. I'll always love you, Gabe, but you don't love me." She lowered her eyes and felt the tears fill them.

"What? No, Alana, that's not true." He grabbed her upper arm and stepped closer.

"Sure it's true, Gabe. If you loved me the way I love you, then your scars, your limp, your handicaps, and your fears that everyone would think you were a failure wouldn't matter because they wouldn't hold water to the power of our love. But you stopped believing."

"No. No, I didn't stop believing. I wanted what was best for you."

She snorted. "Well, guess what, you dumb-ass jarhead. You were wrong. You don't know what's best for me because, if you did, then you would have figured it out that it's you."

His eyes widened, and he looked at the others, and then he looked her over.

"Ah fuck it." He gripped a handful of her blouse, pulled her toward him, and kissed her.

* * * *

Gabe felt the tears in his eyes, and he didn't even care if he cried in front of his brothers. He loved this woman with all his heart. He wished he had done things differently and allowed her the opportunity to support him. But he was scared, just as he still was now for when she would see his scars, his injuries, and the pain he was constantly in.

But right now, all he could do was enjoy everything she was willing to give to him so freely still. Starting with the taste of her kisses, the feel of her sexy body in his arms and against his body. They were moaning and thrusting their hips against one another when he realized he had already dropped the cane and had Alana pressed up against the wall in the kitchen. He ran his hands under her skirt to her ass and squeezed and kneaded her flesh. He devoured her moans and pressed her snugger against the wall as he removed one hand from her ass and cupped her breast. He pulled from her lips.

"God, baby, I missed this body. I missed these breasts and the smell of your shampoo. You were right about everything. I fucked up. Tell me what to do to make it up to you. Tell me how to fix it."

She grabbed his cheeks between her hands and held his gaze.

"Make love to me, Gabe. Ignite that flame, that connection we always had and draw from that strength. I never left you. I was always there. I'm here now, and so are you."

She kissed him on the mouth, and then he turned to look at the others.

"We'll leave you two alone," Jaxon said.

Alana began to speak, but Gabe interrupted her.

"No, we'll all make love to our woman together," he said, and Jaxon, Geno, Jeb, and Gator looked from Gabe to Alana.

"You want us too?" Jaxon asked.

"Yes, and I want you to ruin me for any other men but the five of you."

Gabe raised one eyebrow at her as she chuckled.

"Just take me to bed before I chicken out."

Jaxon chuckled, and Gabe looked at him.

He didn't need to say the words. Jaxon opened his arms, and Alana went willingly. Gabe watched her walk away with the others. Gator smiled at him.

"You better not fuck this up. If I were her, I would have never given your sorry ass a second shot."

"I think you were hoping she would go tell me to fuck myself."

Gator smirked. "No way. Making love to Alana is going to alter all our lives and bring us closer than any mission, any danger, or adventures we ever had. We all need one another, Gabe, just some of us a little more than others."

Gabe thought about that as they both followed the others upstairs. It seemed his buddies had their insecurities as well. Alana was going to be the angel belonging to all of them, not just his.

* * * *

Jaxon set Alana's feet down on the rug in front of the king-sized bed. He took her to his room because he was the one carrying her and he was the leader of this group of hardheaded Marines.

He cupped her cheeks and stared down into her eyes as the others trickled in behind them.

"You've got one hell of a set on you for a woman," he teased.

She squinted. "What exactly does that mean, commander?"

He smirked then gave her lips a quick kiss. He let his lips linger by hers again.

"It means I'm impressed with the daughter of a Marine. Your father would be proud."

He kissed her deeply, and she wrapped her arms around his midsection as she kissed him back.

He felt her jerk slightly, and he knew the others were there. They were joining in one at a time.

"Baby, I can't wait to sink my cock into your sweet, wet pussy. Are you sure you're ready for all of us?" Geno asked her as he massaged her shoulders then ran his hands down her arms to the front of her blouse and began removing her clothing.

Jaxon released her lips, and she moaned a "yes."

He reached for her skirt and pushed it down. Together he and Geno helped her out of her clothing. Now she stood there in a thin, tiny, black lace thong and her matching bra.

"I would have thought you were more the pretty, pink lace type of woman when it came to undergarments," Geno teased her as he slowly pushed her panties down and off of her.

She looked over her shoulder, giving Geno a sassy expression.

"If I knew I was going to have sex with all of you tonight, then I would have worn my cherry-red set. Or maybe my plum-purple set or the green one."

"You have a lot of fancy panties and bras, do ya?" Geno asked then leaned forward and suckled her neck.

Simultaneously, Jaxon took the opportunity to stroke her pussy. He pressed her legs wider and ran a finger along her pussy lips then up into her channel.

"Yes," she replied to Jaxon's ministrations and Geno's question.

"That's a shame you won't be needing any of them."

"I won't?" she asked, not understanding Geno. He and Jaxon chuckled as well as Jeb, Gator, and Gabe.

"Honey, you'll be filled with cock in every hole so often there'll be no need for undergarments," Gator told her.

"Yeah, we'll only rip them off of you anyway," Jeb added.

"Oh God." She moaned.

"Can you handle us together, or should we take you one at a time?" Jaxon thought to ask her.

"It's been so long, and you've all gotten me so aroused right now. I want all of you any way you want me. Just please take me soon. I can't stand it," she confessed, which made Jaxon's cock only get harder.

"That's an order I'm sure we're more than capable of completing." He lifted her up and carried her toward the bed. Geno was standing by the bed, stroking his cock. He pulled her into his arms and kissed her deeply as Jaxon undressed.

Geno released her lips and ran his hand down her arm to her hand. He brought it to his cock, and she covered what she could with her hand. She looked so scared that Jaxon chuckled at her innocence and youth.

"Just breathe, Alana. We'll be sure to get you all wet and ready."

Geno smirked as he covered her hand over his shaft and moved it back and forth.

"I know I'm big, baby, but you can handle it. You're meant for me. For all of us."

Jaxon ran his hands along her hips to her ass. He let his fingers slide between the globes of her butt then up to her spine.

"You're got one hell of an ass. We're going to claim that, too, tonight."

She turned toward him, and Geno chuckled as she released her hold on his shaft to lock gazes with Jaxon.

He cupped her breasts and brought her closer to his naked body. His cock tapped against her belly.

"I'm betting this ass never had a cock in it. Am I right, doll?"

Jaxon was so turned on right now even his words and the casual way he teased his Alana shocked him. And she was his. Was going to be his and his team's once they all made love to her tonight.

She shook her head. "Yes. I've never done that before."

"That's hot," Jeb stated from across the room. He, Gator, and Gabe had their shirts off and were wearing only their dress pants.

Jaxon laced his fingers under her chin and tilted her head up toward him.

"You trust us, don't you, Alana?"

"Yes."

He smiled at how quickly she answered. "You want to be part of this team? Part of us?" Jaxon asked.

"Yes."

"Then offer this body up to us." He leaned forward and kissed her then turned her around to face the others. Geno joined them and watched her as he stroked his cock and her breathing increased.

* * * *

Alana didn't know how to react to this, to Jaxon and his commanding ways. All she knew was that when she turned around and saw Gabe, Geno, Jeb, and Gator watching her, she wanted to please them all.

Jaxon had one strong arm wrapped around her waist, and he ran his other hand along her thigh to her inner groin.

She shivered, almost panicking and covering herself in embarrassment. She suddenly worried about how her body looked to them. They had incredible bodies, made of steel from intense training, and those damn Marine capabilities made her stay right where she was. Alana hadn't realized there was a part of her that needed to be controlled and ordered to please. She knew she had some submissive tendencies, just by the way she reacted to their orders and commanding tone, but this, this brought submission to a whole new level. It was five against one.

Jaxon's palm splayed snug along her belly and hipbone. He didn't need to use much pressure. The man was ultra strong, and his arms felt so good she would be a fool to pull away.

"Open for me," Jaxon whispered against her neck and ear.

She panted. She felt so aroused, but she did as he asked, and she parted her thighs. Her eyes roamed to Gabe first. Gabe looked fierce, and then Gator licked his lips, his eyes on her cunt. Jeb kept his arms crossed, and his eyes were glued to hers as if ready to challenge her or reprimand her if she disobeyed. Why she felt like doing that just to make Jeb react she didn't know, but then Jaxon moved his palm lower over her abdomen and straight to her pussy. He pressed a finger to her cunt.

She tilted her head back and moaned.

"That's right, baby, put your leg up on the bed. Show them your pussy. They're going to claim that pussy tonight just like I am."

"Oh God, Jaxon." She was shaking she was so aroused. She felt her pussy leak, and then Jaxon cupped her breasts and pinched her nipple.

"Oh."

"Do it, " he ordered, and she did. She raised her foot up onto the thick wooden bed frame, instantly becoming off balance and feeling the cool air against her heated folds.

His finger drew circles over her clit then down lower to her anus.

"Oh."

"That's a good girl. You're going to get rewarded right now. Isn't that right, Geno?"

Jaxon's commanding voice put an edge of passion and excitement in the air. Geno fell to his knees in front of her, gripped her thigh and her ass, and licked her cunt with vigor.

Jaxon had removed his fingers and was cupping and massaging her breasts, stimulating her body as she tilted her head back and moaned. It was pure torture but felt so good. Every bit of it felt incredible. She relished the feel of masculine hands gripping her much smaller frame. Fingers over hipbones, a strong tongue licking, circling over her clit as Jaxon's hands massaged and manipulated her breasts.

She moaned and tightened and felt her body react and then her mind wish for more of this pleasurable torture.

Geno lashed his tongue at her pussy lips and suckled her clit, sending a shock of arousal through to her core, and making her wiggle and squirm. Her leg shook, and Geno pushed a finger up into her cunt as he slurped and stroked her over and over again. He was thrusting a finger in and out of her as he ate at her cream while Jaxon held one arm around her waist, keeping her upright while using his other hand to stimulate her nipple.

"Oh Please. Please."

Jaxon egged her on. "Don't tell me this is too much for you, doll. Hell, I'll be real disappointed."

"No. Not too much." She panted, and her voice grew deeper. "I need more," she said in challenge, and he chuckled low against her ear as he nibbled her lobe. She felt the chills run over her flesh as Geno continued to stroke and lick her.

Jaxon began to lower down, and she was forced to hold on to Geno's shoulders so she wouldn't lose her balance. She gasped, and then she moaned when she felt Jaxon lick down her spine and between her ass cheeks to her anus.

"Oh God!" she cried out.

The moment his finger penetrated her anus, Alana screamed. She panted and moaned until Gator was there in front of her, cupping her cheeks.

"Hold on, baby. God, you look like a fucking goddess." He kissed her deeply and plunged his tongue into her mouth as Jaxon fingered her ass and Geno fingered her pussy.

Gator was so big and masculine that his hands encased her face and her head. She moaned and panted, trying to hold his gaze, but her body was beginning to erupt in pleasure. "Gator. Gator please," she begged of him but didn't know what she was begging for.

She felt very tight, as if she should have come already, but it had been so long, and she was over stimulated.

"My turn."

She heard Jeb's voice and then felt Geno's mouth and finger leave her cunt, only to be replaced by Jeb's. He stroked her pussy then nipped at her clit.

"Oh you're so fucking sweet. Hot damn, woman, I can't wait to sink my cock into this cunt. Are you on the pill or do we need condoms?"

"On birth control," she whispered.

"Hot damn. Then there'll be nothing but skin against skin. We're clean, baby. Got tested as routine a few months back," he added.

"I need a taste. I'm going to get lost deep inside this tight, wet pussy. I can't wait."

"Yes, Jeb, please," she begged.

Jaxon pulled his finger from her ass, and Jeb pulled from her pussy and sucked her breast while Gator helped lower her leg from the bed. She was literally shaking as they lifted her up and placed her onto the thick, soft comforter.

In a flash, Jaxon was there between her legs, aligning his cock with her pussy.

"Tell me you want us."

"I want you. All of you. Now," she demanded in desperation.

Jaxon gave a smug smirk and, in one swift motion lifted her up and tossed her onto her belly.

"Jaxon!" she screamed, half pissed and half aroused by his move and need for constant control.

He spread her thighs and pressed his legs between hers to widen them and chuckled.

"Someone needs to learn real fast who's in charge in the bedroom."

Smack.

"Oh."

She hadn't expected the smack to her ass or the instant cream that shot from her cunt. She was done for, finished, and was no way going to be able to handle all their personalities. Geno's dirty talk, Jaxon's authoritative control, and Gator's demands.

Smack.

"Please, Jaxon. Please."

"Are you ready to be a good girl?"

"Yes, yes, please. I need you. I'm desperate."

"She sure is. Damn, she's leaking like a broken faucet," Geno told Jaxon.

Smack.

"I love this ass. I'm going to love claiming that next."

Jaxon's statement made her shiver with anticipation. Having five lovers meant her body was fair game in all ways. Surprisingly, that didn't scare her but made her feel empowered.

He lifted her hips, aligned his cock with her pussy from behind, and slowly pushed into her cunt.

Alana moaned and widened her thighs. She gripped the comforter as she moaned. Jaxon was so thick and big. She wanted him deep inside her, taking away that ache that was bringing tears to her eyes. His spanking seemed to only intensify the feelings, and she felt mad with craziness.

"Fuck, you're so tight. Let me in, baby. I don't want to hurt you." He grunted and wiggled, pulled back, and slowly pushed a little deeper as he massaged her ass cheeks and lifted her hips, working his cock deeper into her cunt.

In and out he eased his thick, hard cock into her tight, dormant pussy until finally he was all the way in. They both sighed in relief, and Jaxon moaned.

"Holy fuck, you're a fucking fantasy. You're so tight and small. I'm not going to last. Fuck." He grunted and eased out then thrust back in.

"Jaxon, faster. Please go faster," she told him, and it seemed to send him over the edge.

He pulled back on her hips, spread her wider, and thrust into her pussy from behind in fast, deep strokes. She screamed and came hard, losing her voice and her breath. Jaxon followed, thrusting, panting, and then holding himself within her, shaking in the aftereffects of their lovemaking.

Jaxon eased out of her, kissing along her shoulders and back as he pulled out. Geno was there to lift her up and place her on top of him. He ran his hands along her back then over her ass. She moaned and kissed his neck then suckled his skin. As achy as she felt, she wanted more. She wanted to make love to all of them tonight and to seal this relationship they were starting.

"Baby, that feels so good. Are you okay? Do you need a minute?" Geno asked as Jaxon ran his hands along her ass cheeks then lowered down to kiss each cheek.

"You're incredible, sweetness, and you're mine now." He kissed her nose, and she smiled a giddy, silly smile in response to his possessive words.

Geno and his sexy brown eyes held her gaze.

"I need you, baby. But I want to make sure that you feel okay. We're all very big, and you're so delicate and small." He traced his finger along her jaw, and the adoration and care in his eyes did her in.

She was touched by his words but also felt compelled to prove to him that she could handle five lovers, even though she wasn't sure herself.

"I need you too." She kissed his mouth then his chin, down his neck and chest all the way to his cock. Without hesitation she pulled the tip into her mouth and gripped his shaft, rubbing, pumping in sync to her strokes.

"Oh fuck, baby, that just isn't fair." He moaned and spread his thighs wider. She felt the second set of hands on her ass and tightened a moment. But then came the stroke of a finger to her pussy from behind and then Jeb's voice.

"Oh you're a wonderful surprise, doll. A lot more than we expected." Jeb thrust a finger up into her cunt.

Geno ran his hands along her breasts, tweaking the nipples, pulling and tugging on her flesh.

Jeb ran his finger back and forth over her cunt, and she was so stimulated that she dripped with cream.

"I'm going to fuck this ass while Geno fucks this wet, tight pussy. What do you think about that?" Jeb asked.

She moaned and nodded, sucking Geno harder until he gripped her hair. She released his cock.

"That's it. When I come, I want to be inside of your pussy."

He lifted her higher, and Jeb helped aligned her pussy with Geno's shaft. She sank down onto him, moaning, feeling his thick muscle fill her. Just as her body accustomed to the thick, wide girth of Geno's cock, Jeb pressed something cold and wet to her anus. His one hand held her hip as his fingers penetrated her anus.

"Jeb?"

"It's just a little lube to make sure I don't hurt you. This virgin ass is going to have a thick, hard cock in it momentarily. We don't want you to feel any pain, sweetheart. Only pleasure." He kissed her shoulder then nibbled next to her neck.

Geno thrust upward as Jeb pressed his slick fingers in and out of her anus.

"Oh, Jeb, I'm scared."

She felt fingers touch her chin, and there was Gator. He knelt on the bed, his cock in his hand, his body in all its glory in plain sight for her to see.

"Easy, honey. Look at me. Look at what you do to me."

She licked her lips and felt the desire overtake her fears.

He eased closer as Geno thrust up into her cunt. "Take him into your mouth. Suck him, baby, and show him how desirable he is to you," Geno ordered her.

She swallowed hard then moaned as Jeb thrust his fingers faster.

She opened her mouth and got her first taste of Gator. He was musky, dark, arousing, and she licked and suckled the tip then began to work him into her mouth.

"Sweet mother of God, get in her ass, Jeb, before I come," Geno ordered.

The power she felt was stimulating, and she suddenly felt as if she could handle anything these men dished out to her. Even their demanding, controlling orders in the bedroom.

She felt Gator holding her hair and her head and begin to slowly pull from her mouth then push back in. She felt comfortable with the pace, despite how hard and deep Geno was pushing up into her cunt.

She moaned against Gator's shaft.

"Oh hell, baby, slow down," he told her, and that seemed to only arouse her more. Between the feel of Geno's cock thrusting up into her pussy and—

She moaned deeply as Jeb pressed against her puckered hole. His cock eased into her ass and began to slide deeper and deeper until she lost her breath and almost gagged on Gator's cock.

Her instinct was to pull forward, but Geno was thrusting upward, holding himself deep within her pussy, and Gator kept his hands gripped in her hair and his cock in her mouth.

She wanted to scream when Jeb whispered into her hair and against her shoulder.

"Let me in, baby. Come one now. You're going to love this. You're our woman now. Give us all of you as we give all of us to you."

He licked her skin and suckled in just the right spot, making her moan and go weak. Jeb's cock thrust all the way into her ass, and he grunted and moaned louder.

"That's it, Alana. Let go and let us love you," Geno told her.

"Fuck, I can't take it. I can't take her mouth," Gator said and began to move faster into her mouth.

She felt herself begin to let go as his cock grew thicker and thicker, and then he moaned and shot his seed down her throat. She sucked and slurped, being sure to lick him clean with Gator moaning then pulling out from her mouth before falling back to the bed.

"She's a damn seductress. Holy fuck," Gator exclaimed.

"She sure the hell is," Jeb said, and he and Geno began to move in sync, thrusting in and out of her body faster and faster.

"Come with us, Alana. Come with us now," Jeb ordered.

The bed was rocking, Alana was moaning and trying to keep up when she screamed another release as Geno and Jeb roared at the same time. She gasped at the fullness and the feel of them releasing their seed in her body before she fell against Geno's chest.

She could hardly move as the men dislodged themselves from her body and strong arms lifted her up off the bed.

"Oh God, I can't move," she whispered against Gator's chest.

He chuckled and carried her into the bathroom.

"A nice hot shower and you'll be good to go."

The spray of the water felt good against her skin. But Gator's hands washing her, lathering the soap and massaging the suds over her breasts, and even over her anus, made her feel another burst of energy. She'd stared to lower as the water cascaded over her body, removing remnants of the soapy suds, when Gator gripped her shoulders.

"No fucking way. That mouth of yours is a lethal weapon."

He pulled her back up and into his arms, kissing her deeply. A moment later she felt the cool tile against her back and ass, and then his cock pressed between her pussy lips.

"Tell me you want me," he said, holding back from penetrating her as he held her gaze, his dark blue eyes demanding and macho.

She ran her hands along his wide, muscular shoulders and shivered as she tried to press closer so he would push his cock into her and ease the ache building in her core.

He gripped her body and gave it a little shake.

"Tell me." He nipped her chin and licked her neck then nipped her chin again. He was wild. She ran her fingers through his crew cut hair and gripped him as he licked and suckled her skin.

"I want you, Gator. Really badly."

She covered his mouth with hers and plunged her tongue deeply in exploration. He kissed her back with just as much hunger and vigor as he pushed the tip of his cock between her pussy lips and filled her in one, mind-altering stroke.

She nearly pulled from his mouth to gasp, but he held her tight, pressed her body against the tile wall, and thrust again and again. The water slapped and splashed between their bodies, and their skin slid against one another as they rocked, thrust, and moaned.

She tried climbing higher up him, wanting his cock even deeper as she held him and kissed him back with control. She massaged then pinched his nipples, feeling the pectoral muscles beneath her palms arouse her further. That set Gator off, and he pulled her hands from his chest, placed them above her head on the wall, and began a series of hard, fast strokes into her pussy.

"Gator! Gator!"

She screamed his name and exploded around his shaft. But he kept going, thrusting, stroking, rocking against her, filling her to her womb and claiming her in an almost animalistic manner. She loved it. It made her feel wild, and she counter-rocked her hips against his.

"Mine. You're fucking mine." He yelled so loudly and deeply that she gasped as he came, filling her with his seed.

"God, you're going to be my everything, sweetness. My everything," he confessed as he hugged her tightly and held himself within her as they both calmed their breathing and relished the aftermath of their loving encounter.

* * * *

Gabe was pacing the room and running his fingers through his hair. He could hear them moaning and Gator raising his voice and fucking Alana in the shower. His own dick was so rock solid hard right now that he wasn't sure he could move, never mind make love to Alana.

And how was he going to balance his weight on his knees as he made love to her when his legs were weak? He could barely hold his own body weight and needed the fucking cane.

"Fuck," he said under his breath. He felt the hand on his shoulder and turned to see Jeb there.

"We're not going to leave your side. We'll help you."

"I can't do this. I won't even be able to hold myself up and make love to her like a real man should."

"Bullshit. Stop fucking focusing on your injuries and focus on what Alana does to you. Focus on how it feels to kiss her, touch her, and hold her in your arms. Just take your time," Geno added.

"We can leave if it makes it easier," Jaxon suggested.

Gabe shook his head.

It was so hard to admit his weaknesses, and his fears, but these were his brothers. They were the reasons why he'd lived these last three years. They'd taken care of him and made sure that he healed once he was released from the military hospital in Germany. They were his support network, and they all had just made love to his woman, to Alana. It was only right to have them here so, if he failed, they could take over and satisfy her needs and desires.

"If I fail. If I can't satisfy her, help me," he whispered, holding Jaxon's gaze. He could see the emotions in all their eyes.

"You won't need us. Alana is special in many ways. You'll find the will, the need to become one with her. You won't need us. Just remember the bond you already share. That's a bond you've allowed us all to be part of, and it's fucking powerful." Jaxon moved toward one of the big single chairs and took a seat.

Geno and Jeb walked over to two other chairs and sat while Gabe pulled off his shirt.

His fingers shook as he thought about his scars and the deep gash of missing flesh. He realized that he didn't want to be ugly to her. He wanted her to find him handsome and capable, her knight in shining armor. Well, maybe a bit tarnished and banged up, but still capable.

The moment he felt the hand on his shoulder, he froze in place.

Alana.

She gently ran the palms of her hands along his back then pressed her lips to his skin, even over the scars of battle wounds. He was tense, uptight, filled with anxiety about pleasing her and making love to her after all this time when she shocked him. She wrapped her arms around him from behind and hugged him.

"I love you, Gabe."

He swallowed hard, turned around, and pulled her against his chest. He held her tight and ran his hands along her body and pushed the towel covering her away from her flesh.

He cupped her cheeks, leaned down on shaky legs, and kissed her deeply. She gave so freely, his angel, his goddess, his woman.

She ran her hands along his waist and up his chest, and he shivered from the deep sensations that filled him. He pulled from her lips and held her gaze. Alana's green eyes sparkled with unshed tears, and she smiled.

"Make love to me, Gabe. Claim me like your team has so we can be one."

Her statement, her understanding and description of this joining, enlightened him and brought a surge of desire and determination to his soul.

"I plan on it, baby. Be patient with me. I'm weak," he said, and she shook her head.

"You're not weak. You're strong, you're a survivor, and you're a Marine. My Marine. Let me in. I'll help you, just open up."

She slid down his chest, licking and kissing his skin as her palms worked over his belly muscles and then began to undo his belt and dress pants. He held his breath when she pushed them down, revealing his scars, his battered, destroyed flesh, and she didn't shudder or gasp. No, she did the unexpected, the most courageous, loving thing a woman, his woman, could do. She kissed his wounds.

She hugged his legs and lay her cheek over his damaged, missing flesh and showed him just how big her heart really was.

He felt the tear roll down his cheek, and he quickly wiped it away but not before he locked gazes with his team, emotion in their eyes, understanding, relief, and love. They were going to be a family, one unit, one team, and all because of Alana. She completed them.

Her lips kissed along his thighs then back up to his cock. He held her shoulders as he stepped out of his clothing, now fully naked before her and, thank God, past the awkwardness of her seeing his scars.

She twirled her tongue around his shaft, taking her time to taste him, arouse him, and get his mind off of everything else but the feel of her mouth on him.

Gabe ran his fingers through her hair and breathed through the pleasure of her strokes. She sucked him thoroughly, moving her head up and down as she massaged his balls and make his dick even harder.

When she pulled her mouth from his cock and began to press him back against the bed, he knew what she intended. She was going to ride him, take away that worry he had of not being able to hold himself on top and make love to her.

He fell back onto the bed, and she climbed upon him, her breasts so beautiful and full. Lovelier, more womanly than he recalled from years ago.

"You're so beautiful, baby. You're the most beautiful woman, person, I've ever known."

He cupped her hair and neck and drew her closer for a kiss. A kiss that grew deeper and more desperate with every stroke of his tongue.

He thrust his hips, wanting more of her, and she pulled from his mouth, gasping, taking unsteady breaths.

He cupped her breasts, leaned up, and licked along the nipple, first on the right and then to the left before pushing them together and licking the deep, cleavage of her breasts.

She was going to align her pussy with his cock, and he gripped her hips.

He held her gaze, and she looked down at him, her long brown hair covered her breasts and her eyes glistening with tears. She was feeling the depth of these emotions they shared, and he adored her.

"I want to taste you," he admitted, and her cheeks turned a nice shade of pink. He winked at her.

She began to lift higher, and he used his hands to maneuver her ass and cunt over his face. He inhaled, and her scent of soap, honey, and her unique nectar made him feel instantly hungry.

He licked at her pussy lips, her cream dripping and ready like a meal for his pleasure and enjoyment. He twirled his tongue around her clit and tugged then suckled it. The sound of her moaning filled the room. He pressed a finger up into her channel, making her cream some more.

"Oh Gabe. Gabe," she moaned.

"Come on my face, baby. Give me more," he ordered, and she moaned and came. He licked and sucked her cream, and then he lifted her higher.

"I need you now. I can't wait. I'm going to come, baby."

"Inside me, Gabe. Please come inside of me."

He pulled her closer and kissed her deeply. She aligned his cock with her cunt and lowered over him, taking his cock into the depths of her tight, hot pussy.

It was like heaven. Like nothing he'd ever experienced before. How could he have forgotten how perfect he felt when he was deep inside of Alana like this? Why had he suppressed such powerful memories? All because he was scared? Afraid she wouldn't love him? He had been so stupid, but Alana had been stronger. She never gave up on him, and he would never give up on her, on any of them ever again.

A bond, a connection, a power stronger then the tests of time, larger than life itself.

"Alana."

Jaxon, Geno, and Jeb were right. Alana had the power to destroy any of his reservations and fears. All because he loved her.

He rolled her to her back, making her gasp and drawing the attention of his brothers. He thrust into her and lifted to his knees, the ache not as strong as the desire to claim Alana as his woman again and not as strong as his need to fuck her.

He thrust his hips, pushing his cock in and out of her, and pushed her thighs wider and higher.

He was sweating and beginning to shake, and he knew he wasn't physically going to last much longer, despite his desperate need to show her he was still a man. Her man.

"I never stopped loving you either, Alana. I'll never hurt you again." he promised, and she cried out his name as she came. He followed, held himself deep in her pussy, and erupted as he let go.

* * * *

Alana awoke surrounded by warmth, and the smell of cologne and soap filled her nostrils. Someone was caressing her hair and her back. Her cheek was pressed against solid muscle, and as she blinked her eyes open, she saw Gabe watching her. Dark black hair, bold brown eyes that seemed brighter than they had been since she'd seen him that day at the estate sale. Her eyes filled with tears, and she hugged him, the fact that he was real and was holding her in bed once again brought on a surge of emotions.

He continued to caress her hair. "I missed you, baby."

She tilted her head up and ran the palm of her hand along his chest.

"I missed you so much too, Gabe."

"I thought I wanted to die, or at least be dead, so I wouldn't have to face anyone."

She lifted up and held herself up, leaning on her elbow.

"What do you mean face everyone? Why? Because you're injured?"

He released an annoyed sigh and tried adjusting his position, cringing from the ache. She ran her palm over his belly and held his gaze.

"Tell me why," she demanded to know.

He ran his hand along her ass as she pulled the sheets to cover her breasts.

He looked away.

"I didn't want you to see me like this. A failure, a weak invalid who can't even walk without a fucking cane."

"No Gabe. Why would you think that? How could you see yourself as a failure when you're a hero."

He shook his head. "I'm not a hero. I'm all fucked up, and you deserve better. How could I ask a beautiful, perfect woman like you to take me back when you could have perfect men like the others?"

She held his gaze and processed what he was sharing with her.

"God, I really want to smack some sense into you, Gabe. Are you out of your mind? I love you. Always have, and none of that has changed."

"But your dad came back fine."

"Oh, Gabe, I told you about how my dad suffered with nightmares. He wasn't perfect. Why would you think I would want perfect?"

He pushed the sheets down and away from her breasts then lifted her up and over his hips. He widened his thighs, and she fell forward as he cupped her hair and head, bringing her closer to his lips.

"Because you're perfect." He kissed her, and Alana held on to him as they made love again and moved another step closer to putting the past behind them.

Chapter 5

Sarah Lark finished working at the salon and made her way down the street to the parking lot. She was exhausted. It had been a long day, a long week for that matter, and all she wanted to do was go home to take a nice hot bath.

Her cell phone rang, and she fumbled with her keys to unlock the door as she answered the phone. Using her shoulder to hold her phone as she tossed her purse then bag into the front passenger seat, she heard her friend Elizabeth's excitement.

"Hey, where are you? You're not still working, are you? We're all here at the club."

"Oh God, Elizabeth. I just got off work. I'm getting into my car now."

"You have to come here. The guys are smoking hot."

"You say that all the time. I just don't think I have the energy tonight."

"Oh come on over for one drink. If you don't feel better and can't stay, then leave. But you have come here. It's so much fun, and every one who is anyone is here."

Sarah took a deep breath and released it. "Fine. One drink and then a bubble bath is calling my name."

Fifteen minutes later, and after she finally found a parking spot two small shopping centers away, Sarah walked into the club. Elizabeth was right. It was jam-packed, and there were so many people. She felt encouraged that she'd made the right choice in coming here.

As she approached her friends, she noticed the guys around them, and Elizabeth had been right. There were some smoking-hot guys here.

Everyone greeted her hello, and she was grateful she had worn the skirt and heeled boots to work today. At least she was dressed for the dance hall club scene. Elizabeth handed her a drink, and from there on out, she knew she was not going to be heading home soon.

* * * *

He watched her from afar. Not quite as conservative or beautiful as his Alana, but she would do. He just needed to take off the edge. He was becoming desperate, and the other day in the store he'd nearly lost it. To see Alana with those two men, soldiers, too, just like he was, really angered him. They wanted her. They wanted to fuck her together and make her theirs, but he wasn't going to let that happen.

I saw her first. She's mine.

He clenched his fists then unclenched them, feeling his blood pressure rising and his heart racing with fury. He needed to calm down. Everything had to be perfect when he finally took Alana. He needed practice. Practice arousing a woman, making her beg for mercy then beg for his cock. He couldn't do that right for Alana if he didn't practice first. The other woman hadn't worked out as he planned.

She'd fought him. Called him names and mocked him as if he weren't good enough for her. She suffered the consequences of defying him. Just like this one would if she reacted the same way. No, he needed to do this differently. Gain her trust. Make her like him and accept his advances then begin the training.

He took a deep breath and looked around him. To ensure he wasn't identified if things went awry like with the other woman, he should make this quick. As quick as he could without gaining attention.

"Excuse me."

She turned around and smiled. Soft, sweet, brown eyes not green, but she would do.

"Yes?"

"I saw you from across the room. You looked familiar to me. Are you from Salvation?" he asked her.

"I don't think I've seen you before, but yes, I work around here."

"Maybe that's where I've seen you. I would never forget a pretty face. Do you work for the newspaper?"

She blushed and shyly looked away. He knew he had big muscles, was pretty attractive, as he got looks often. But he played off shy too.

"No, I work at the salon."

"Well, I don't think that's where I've seen you before."

"Sarah, we're going to dance. Are you coming?" a friend of hers asked, interrupting the conversation. He shot her a look then recovered quickly and winked.

"I'm sorry to bother you. I'll let you get back to your friends," he said in a sad voice. She placed her hand on his arm, and he bit his cheek. No woman touched him or showed control over him.

"Stay. I'm not in the mood for dancing," she said, and her friend shrugged and walked away.

He spent the rest of the time courting her. He gave her small compliments and made up a story about himself and where he came from. The more they engaged in conversation, the more he found her to be similar to Alana, and he knew that she would do just fine.

As the night went on, he made his move as she said she was tired and wanted to head home. He offered to walk her out, and she looked for her friends, but none of them seemed to be around.

He offered her assistance.

The moment he got to her car, he knew this was meant to be. His van was only two vehicles away, and he had knocked out the parking lot light above on his way in earlier. It seemed that fate was on his side after all.

"God, it's so dark out here. I think one of the lights is out," she said.

"Well then, I'm glad I walked you out. That could be dangerous."

He placed his hand at her lower back and looked around as she searched for her keys. She gave him a smile, and then he reached into his pocket for the small syringe.

"Well, it was nice meeting you."

"It was nice meeting you too. The night is young. Maybe we could continue the good time we've been having?" he asked.

"I don't think I have the energy. Not tonight. But maybe I'll see you here again? Maybe this Friday? We could meet," she suggested.

He had her. But he couldn't wait a week. He needed training.

"Why wait when we can have tonight?" He stepped closer and went to kiss her, but she pressed her hands against his chest and stopped him.

"I don't know you. I'm sorry but maybe another time." She turned him down, and he panicked.

"Not another time. Tonight."

She went to move away from him, and he pulled her close then stuck her in the neck with the syringe. She gasped, and he pulled her close. He heard voices, turned, and saw two guys and a woman heading out of the club and toward where they stood. He improvised like a good soldier should.

He pressed her body against the car and held her close as he kissed her. She was sweet and pliant in his arms. She would be perfect.

"Get a room, buddy," one of the guys said, and the woman they were with reprimanded him. "Leave them alone. Let's go."

They got into the car right beside Sarah's and pulled out of the parking lot. He watched them leave and released Sarah's lips then dragged her toward the van. He'd done it. He was successful. Now the training would begin.

* * * *

"Come here," Jaxon said to Alana as she walked into the kitchen dressed in a long button-down dress shirt. His burgundy one.

She came to him willingly, and his heart raced with adoration for her. He pulled her close and kissed her deeply until she was flush against his body.

"Are you feeling okay?"

He tilted her head back as he held her cheeks and head between his hands, staring down into her gorgeous green eyes.

"Yes," she whispered.

He ran a hand along her ass, squeezing it and pulling her snugger against his chest.

She looked concerned.

"What's wrong?"

"I think Gabe overdid it. He asked me to give him some time while he took a shower."

He understood her concern.

He ran his hand under her shirt and against her ass, realizing she was wearing only her thong.

"He'll be fine. After all, with a body like yours, he's bound to lose control again. We all will."

She hugged him, surprising him, as his heart felt full with instant adoration.

"Hey, I'm serious. He'll be fine," he told her, cupping her cheeks. He could see the tears of concern in her eyes.

Her stomach growled.

"How about something to eat?"

"I'm starving."

"Well, you and Gabe kind of missed out on dinner last night."

"That was your fault too," she said, pushing to change the subject of Gabe's condition just like he was.

"Just wait. You may miss it again tonight."

"Jaxon, I'll need to go home soon. I have work tomorrow."

He felt an ache in his belly. He didn't want her to leave, but then he saw Geno sneak up behind her, wrap his arms around her waist, and lift her up into the cradle position in his arms.

Alana gasped.

"Geno."

Jaxon could see her ass as Geno lifted her up into his arms.

"You're not going anywhere. I'm taking you prisoner."

She placed her hand on his chest then gave him a light slap. She tried to push the shirt down to cover her ass.

Gator whistled as he joined them.

"Put me down," she stated.

"Hot damn, mamma, I can get used to coming down to the kitchen and seeing you flashing your ass."

"Gator," she reprimanded and still tried to cover up, but Geno set her down on the kitchen table and lowered her down. She pressed her hands against his chest.

"Geno." She said his name in a tone that meant business, and Jaxon chuckled.

Geno reached under her shirt and cupped her breast.

"I know exactly what I want for breakfast."

"Lunch," Gator teased, taking a seat at the table and gliding his hand up along Alana's thigh.

"Gator, stop that. Geno, let me up," she stated, and Geno manipulated her breasts.

"First things first." Geno pushed her shirt up to her neck and leaned down to feast on her left breast. Jaxon chuckled as Gator lifted the shirt up and leaned forward to feast on her right breast.

She grabbed their hair and heads and held on as she moaned and tried to reprimand them.

"What do we have here?" Jeb joined them.

"Oh God. Please stop, this isn't fair. It's two against one."

"Four actually," Jaxon said.

"Jaxon, order them to stop. We're on the kitchen table. Someone might come to the door," she carried on, truly feeling embarrassed.

Geno and Gator stopped suckling her breast, and Geno pulled her shirt back down.

"Ain't no one ever going to see you naked but the five of us. And get yourself ready, woman. I, for one, plan on having you in a lot of places in this house, including this here kitchen table." He pressed a finger over her mound and against her panties, making her wiggle and screech at him.

Gator laughed, and Geno lifted her up, cupped her cheeks, and kissed her deeply.

As Geno pulled from her mouth, Jaxon thought she might reprimand Geno again or maybe even give him a smack against his chest, but instead, she wrapped her arms around him and hugged him tight.

Geno looked stunned as he locked gazes with Jaxon then Gator and Jeb. His buddy looked incredibly happy.

* * * *

Alana watched Jaxon and Geno cooking breakfast and admired their bodies over the mug of her hot cup of coffee. Gator was making the toast, and Jeb was looking at his laptop, checking out the latest news. It was apparently a morning ritual that the others shared with her. She couldn't help but admire their sexy bodies and the way it felt to be surrounded by four men she'd made love to last night.

She looked up toward the ceiling, worried about Gabe. He hadn't come down yet, and he should have by now. She pulled her lower lip between her teeth and contemplated heading back upstairs to check on him. She put her mug down and ran the palms of her hands down her thighs and over the bit of material from Jaxon's shirt. That was another thing. She was practically naked, and they were all fully dressed except for their feet. No one was wearing any shoes.

She sensed her body's reaction to the men and couldn't help but think about last night. She had let them all make love to her. Gabe had watched them all make love to her before he took her last. It was kind of overwhelming. They were big men, very dominant and controlling. She had been on her own, taking care of herself for quite some time. Would their need for control cause a problem in the future?

If she'd learned one thing last night, she was definitely a submissive who enjoyed being ordered around by these men. She wanted to please them. To give them all of her heart and her soul. She began to feel a little panicked. She'd given them her heart and soul last night. What if they left her like Gabe had?

She felt the tears sting her eyes, and she quickly stood up.

"Alana, breakfast is ready," Jaxon told her.

She looked up at him, locked gazes with his blue eyes, and knew that he could tell she was upset.

"Alana?"

She turned away. "I'll be right back. I just need to use the bathroom." She hurried out of there and could hear the scraping of a chair then footsteps. She quickly entered the bathroom and closed the door. She locked it and a moment later, as the tears rolled down her cheeks and an anxiety attack began, she heard the knock.

She gasped.

"Alana, are you okay?" Jaxon asked.

She tried to speak, but her mind kept whirling over the possibilities of how terrible this whole ménage relationship could end.

"Answer me, Alana, or I'll break down the door."

"Fine. Need a minute," she barked out and then turned to look at herself in the mirror as she gripped the sink and counter.

Her face was pale, her eyes filled with tears as worry filled her heart.

Where had all her self-confidence gone? When had she decided to overanalyze the situation and freak out? And she was definitely freaking out. Jaxon, Geno, Jeb, Gator, and Gabe were five very large, capable men. In that large kitchen with four of them, she'd felt exposed, outnumbered, vulnerable… and that was it. She was feeling vulnerable.

All this time, over the years, she trained herself to be so self-sufficient and to not take any orders or direction from anyone but herself. She had to live her life. She had to make the mistakes, and she'd had to survive on her own after losing her parents and losing Gabe. By giving into this attraction, this sexual need and pull to these five men, was she giving up that freedom to choose, to live her life, and to do as she wanted?

Were they instantly going to make demands on her? She loved the way they made love to her. She wouldn't mind those sexual demands, but what about the other stuff?

"Alana, open up. We're worried," Jeb said.

"I'm fine, Jeb. Just give me a minute. I'll meet you in the kitchen."

"No, you'll open the door right now," Jaxon demanded.

She felt her heart race. He was fierce and demanding. It concerned her but aroused her more.

She wiped her eyes and took and an unsteady breath. She could do this. She could have breakfast with them, maybe make love to them again, and then head home to her cottage and continue her normal routine.

Her small, lonely cottage, where she was going to sleep alone and dream of them and wish they were with her. But she couldn't do that. She had to maintain her control, her independence, and, of course, her sanity.

With that last bit of pep talk, she unlocked the door, and Jaxon stood there, arms crossed, with an angry expression, and she did what anyone would do in such a situation. She tried walking right by him.

His hand touched hers, and she froze in place.

Alana gulped and then tilted her head way up to give him a soft smile.

It didn't work. He held her gaze with a firm expression that was all Jaxon.

God, he's so sexy. I love this man.

Her eyes widened at her own thoughts. It was instant. She fell in love with him in one night of lovemaking. She was in love with all of them. How stupid could she be? This was how she'd lost control and fallen into a pool of depression when Gabe left her.

"Alana, I don't know what's going through your pretty little head right now, but I suggest we discuss it."

Jaxon. Damn controlling leader of his entire team and now her too? She couldn't allow this. She couldn't succumb to his sexual appeal, masculinity, and authoritative demeanor and crumble into a weak love-struck dope.

She pulled her hand from his. It was best to not confront him or cause an argument she would surely lose. She smiled softly.

"I'm fine, Jaxon. Just tired and hungry. Why don't we go eat?"

She began walking. He stopped her and pressed her up against the wall as he cupped one cheek with his palm so gently and eyes filled with passion. His other hand wrapped around her waist possessively, and he swept down and kissed her.

In that moment, as her lips parted to his need for control, an act she was more than likely going to have to get used to, she gave in. She allowed the feel of his arms, the gentleness of his compassion to overtake her. There was no turning back. The fire, the connection, and power between them were combustible. She kissed him back, rocked her hips against his, and then felt his hand move lower and press her panties down her thighs.

"Jaxon," she reprimanded, but in actuality, she was utterly turned on and dripping wet.

"I want you. I can't get enough of you," he told her as he lifted her up so she had to wrap her legs around his waist. He maneuvered out of his pants, dropping them to the floor as he pressed her back against the wall so she wouldn't fall.

"You're mine. Do you even realize that?" he asked her as he held her gaze, gripped his cock, and pressed up into her cunt.

She gripped his forearms and gasped at the forceful, sexual invasion.

He thrust fully into her, making her moan.

Jaxon cupped her cheeks between his hands as he rocked his hips back and forth, thrusting into her wet channel and making her hold his complete attention.

"I didn't like that look in your eyes. That uncertain, almost panicked expression. Last night was perfect. From here on out will be perfect because you're meant to be ours."

He kissed her deeply as his words sunk in. Jaxon's ability to see through to her thoughts, to know she was indeed panicking, overwhelmed her with emotion. He thrust in and out of her, and she held on to him, reveling in the feel of his hard, thick cock marking her, claiming her as his woman again and again.

Jaxon was the leader, the man in control of the men, of all of them. It seemed this included her now, and that was something she needed time to process. But for the moment, in this heat of passion, she gave of herself fully. She countered his thrusts, called out his name as she came, and accepted him fully as he exploded inside of her.

"Never be scared of me, of any of us. You come first. You complete us. Life as you know it is about to change."

Her eyes widened, and he kissed her again as he held his cock within her pussy and she battled with her mind's wild thoughts and her body's feeling of completion.

Chapter 6

Gabe and Gator drove Alana home, and Gator wasn't pleased. He wanted Alana with them. He wanted to hold her in his arms in bed and explore her sexy body. He couldn't believe how obsessed he felt after two full days and one night with her. They had fun. They all laughed a little. It was different, strange, but felt good.

As he pulled up into her driveway and looked at the small cottage all dark, his stomach churned with worry. He didn't like her staying here alone. He wanted her with them, but that would not go over well. Jaxon had explained about her odd behavior earlier this morning. He hoped they'd worked her fears or any concerns out of her by all making love to her again and again. But he knew women were fickle sometimes. He just hoped that she wasn't having second thoughts.

Gabe climbed out of the truck, limping and trying not to groan in front of Alana. He'd overdone it, but Gator was certain Gabe didn't regret one second of it.

"The house is so dark. You should have left a light on the other day," Gabe told her, almost reprimanding her. Instead of snapping back at him, she looped her arm through his and walked with him.

"It's okay. I have the two of you to walk me in. Remember, Gabe, I've never been too fond of the dark."

He reached up and paced his palm against her cheek. "You still sleep with a nightlight on?" he asked.

"Yes."

"How about a stuffed animal?" Gator teased her as she released Gabe's arm and unlocked her front door.

"I have something better than a stuffed animal," she said as they entered.

Alana turned on the lights, and Gator checked out the house to make sure it was secure. One glance out the back door to the dark backyard and woods and he felt his concern grow. He didn't know why. He was being so possessive, and he wanted to demand that she stay with them. But that couldn't happen.

* * * *

Gabe followed Alana into her bedroom, where she closed the shades. He looked around and was surprised at all the pictures she had of them and of his parents.

His chest tightened as he took one of the pictures of them as teens leaning next to his beat-up pickup truck, and he smiled.

"God, that truck was such a piece of crap."

"But reliable. We only broke down that one time," she told him.

He remembered that. They'd made good use of being stranded out on the back roads of town at night. She was beautiful then, but now Alana was all woman. Her maturity, classiness, and sex appeal was even greater.

"Oh I remember that, and those tiny purple panties I removed," he said as he pulled her closer to him by her hips. She ran her palms up his chest, and she blushed.

"Figures you would remember that. How about almost getting caught by the local deputy driving by?"

"Harvey couldn't see shit. Besides, he had it bad for you anyway, and there was no way I'd take a chance of him seeing what belonged to me." He squeezed her closer, leaned down, and kissed her.

The feel of her hands running through his hair calmed him and made him feel almost normal. Only Alana had the ability to do that.

"It's all clear and locked up," Gator said, joining them in the bedroom.

"Great. I can't wait to get out of these clothes."

"Well, that's definitely something Gabe and I can help you with," Gator told her, joining them by the bed.

He cupped her cheeks then drew her in for a kiss. Gabe watched Alana reach up and caress Gator's shoulder then neck. She made Gator happy. She made the whole group of them happy.

"Top or bottom, Gabe?" Gator asked as he began to undress Alana.

Gabe undid Alana's skirt, pushing it down and off of her. He saw her bare pussy, thanks to Jaxon, and licked his lips.

"I think I'll take bottom." He stroked his finger over her pussy lips as Gator licked across her nipple.

Gabe undid his pants with one hand and shoved them down as he stroked Alana's cunt. Gator moved behind her, and Gabe could hear him undressing.

"Put one leg up on the bed, doll." Gator gave the order, and she responded immediately.

Gabe sat down, pushed off his pants, and looked at Alana.

Gator was cupping her breasts from behind her.

"Touch your pretty little cunt for us, baby. Gabe wants to see you finger yourself," Gator told her.

Gabe watched her eyes glisten and go big. She looked so damn sexy with one leg up on the bed, her legs wide, her pussy showing. He stroked his own cock as she reached for her clit and began to move her fingers around in a circular motion.

"Alana, you're a goddess," Gabe told her, and she moaned, closed her eyes, and thrust two fingers up her pussy.

She shocked him and Gator when she pulled her fingers out and pressed them to Gabe's lips.

Gator chuckled.

"Full of surprises," he said.

Smack.

She gasped as he gave her ass a smack. "Gator."

"Wait until I tell Jeb, Geno, and Jaxon what you did."

Gabe licked her fingers, sucked them into his mouth, and licked away the cream. Her lips parted, and she brought her foot off the bed, leaned lower, and kissed Gabe. He tried kissing her back, but it seemed Alana wanted to please them both and get Gator wild. She lowered down, took Gabe's cock between her lips, and stuck her ass back against Gator, placing her legs far apart, like Jaxon and Geno had taught her.

"Oh hell, woman, that's fucking hot."

Gator smacked her ass a few more times, and Alana moaned against Gabe's cock.

"Hell, baby, I'm going to come," Gabe said to her.

"Not yet. Wait until we're both inside of her," Gator replied then caressed her ass cheeks and leaned down and prepared her ass for his cock.

Alana moaned and wiggled then lifted up and gasped.

Gator's hands were on her hips, and he was smiling.

"I think you better climb on up there, woman," Gator said, and Alana shot a look over her shoulder at Gator.

"Don't be sassing me, girl. Fuck that cock. Work it up into that pussy of yours and show Gabe you own that cock. Do it, and we'll both make you come so fucking hard you'll remember who owns this ass and pussy."

Smack.

"Oh God, Gator, I can't take the way you talk," she said, almost panting, and Gabe chuckled.

He helped her up onto his lap, and she straddled his hips and took his cock deep.

"Get used to it, doll. I've never seen him like this," Gabe told her, and Alana cried out as Gator thrust into her ass from behind.

Gabe moaned, too, feeling his cock tighten and grow thicker. He could feel the friction between their skin as Gator stroked in and out of her ass.

"Ride him," Gator ordered, and Alana did.

She moaned and cried out as she thrust and rocked on top of him. Gabe grunted and held her hips. He cupped her breasts, pulled on her nipples, and felt himself grow thicker.

"I'm going come, baby," Gabe said.

"Oh God. I feel so tight, so full. I can't take it. Oh God!"

She screamed out her release, and Gabe and Gator thrust up into her. Gabe could feel her hot cream surround his oversensitive cock, and he lost control.

"Alana," he cried out and came.

Behind her, Gator thrust faster and faster, rocking them and the bed before he roared and shook, coming inside of Alana's ass.

"Oh God, I'll never walk the same again," Alana stated and Gabe and Gator chuckled.

They both caressed her body, and Gator massaged her ass and her back and kissed her shoulders and her cheeks. Gabe watched, thrilled at witnessing the love and care Gator had for Alana. He knew that all the guys probably loved her already, and he couldn't ask for anything more than that. They would protect her and care for her if he ever failed to do so.

Gator pulled gently from her ass and gave her ass cheeks a light smack.

"Gator," she reprimanded, reaching back and caressing her ass cheek.

Gabe stretched out as she lifted up, pulling her body from his. Gabe rolled her to her back and kissed her as he held her gaze.

"You'll walk just fine," he said, and she gave him a sassy look as he chuckled.

As Gabe turned toward her pillows on the bed, he saw something sticking out from underneath one.

"Hey, what's this?" he asked.

He held up the army green T-shirt that looked as if it was worn and belonged to a guy. His chest tightened as she pulled it from his hands.

"Nothing," she said.

Gator was pulling his pants on and gave her an angry expression. "Is that a guy's shirt?" he asked.

She sat up and put the shirt on, covering her breasts from their view.

"Alana, who's fucking shirt is that, and what is it doing under your pillow on your bed?" Gabe asked her, getting angry and feeling jealous too.

"It's not what you think. It doesn't belong to some guy. It's…I've had it forever." She hugged herself.

Gabe reached out and touched the shirt.

"Who's is it?" he asked.

"Yeah, who the fuck owns that shirt?" Gator demanded to know.

"You," she said to Gabe, holding his gaze.

He stared at her as his mind tried to process her statement, and it hit him.

"So this is that special thing that you sleep with? My military shirt from before I left for Iraq?"

She gulped and looked from Gator back to Gabe.

"Yes."

He reached out and cupped her cheeks.

"Damn, baby, I'm going to make up for all the pain I caused you. I swear to you, baby. I swear." He kissed her softly, and she hugged him.

"I guess I'll let this slide. Considering," Gator told her.

She pulled back from Gabe and reached out for Gator's hand. She pulled him closer.

"Shut up, Gator, and just kiss me."

Gabe chuckled, and Gator did as Alana said and kissed her. They weren't leaving her tonight. They were staying.

* * * *

Gunner stood outside of the motel room where the crime scene was located. He popped a piece of gum into his mouth, trying to get the taste of death out of his mouth. He looked at Jim and Teddy.

"This is the second fucking dead body, and the wounds, the damage to her, is too similar to that other girl found murdered two weeks ago," Jim said to Gunner.

The coroner was there, the forensic team was finishing up, and Gunner was angry.

"We have to find this sick fuck. I told that forensics team to be extra thorough. The perpetrator has to fuck up somewhere. He did all this damage to that beautiful young woman, and no one heard a fucking thing?"

"It's crazy, but this side of the motel was vacant. It was a weeknight, not the weekend. This motel is almost always booked up Friday to Sunday," Teddy said as he looked at his notes.

"The guy at the front desk doesn't have any info on the person who paid for this room?" Teddy asked Gunner.

"No. The person secured it over the phone and paid cash. He deposited it into the outside mailbox by the office."

"So it was a man?" Jim said.

"That's pretty obvious by the damage done to that girl. But yes, the manager said the person on the phone who booked the room was a man," Gunner told him.

"We have the deputies casing the place and trying to question people. But considering this is a motel, and it seems people aren't willing to even speak to the police, we may have a dead end here," Jim said.

"Yeah, I saw that coming. The manager said that people rent the rooms by the hour too. He doesn't even have enough time to clean them in between, and the people who come here don't care."

"That's fucking disgusting," Teddy replied.

"Tell me about it. Someone must have seen something. I asked the manager to compile a list of all his guests over the last forty-eight hours. We'll start there," Gunner told them.

"We'll take part of the list, too, and apply the pressure. You're right, Gunner. Someone had to have seen this guy and that girl come here last night. Tough shit if they were cheating on someone or just fucking around. This is the second young woman to be murdered around Salvation. That just isn't acceptable," Teddy said.

Gunner looked around him. He had a really bad feeling that this investigation was going to get worse if the body count rose. Someone knew something, and he was going to find them.

* * * *

Alana couldn't believe the workweek had passed so quickly. It was Friday night, and she was working at Casper's and missing her men. She was serving up some beers to several patrons when she overheard them talking about the murders of two young women. Both had been tortured and sexually assaulted then left for dead. She felt so sick to her stomach to hear about something like this happening in Salvation. Everyone was.

As the guys discussed safety measures with a few women who were standing around drinking and enjoying the night, she heard the women's responses and their lack of concern.

"It's not like anything like that would happen to us. We don't hook up with guys we just met," one said.

"What does that mean?" one guy asked.

"They found her body in the motel on Highway 10. Everyone knows that people go there for sex," she said.

The same guy ran his hand around her waist, pulling her back, and rocked his hips back and forth against her ass.

"So you want to go there with me tonight?" he teased her.

"You wish, Donny," she replied, and they all chuckled.

"How about you, gorgeous?" some guy said, turning to Alana. "When do you get off work? Maybe we can check out that motel on Highway 10?"

Before she could reply, Geno came up behind the guy and slapped his hand on the guy's shoulder.

"That's my fucking girlfriend, asshole."

"Oh shit, Geno. I didn't know," Donny replied, stepping back.

"She belongs to us," Jeb added and moved the group out of the way as Jaxon, Gator, and Gabe relocated to their spot by the bar in front of her.

Alana crossed her arms in front of her chest. "Feel better now, Geno?"

"I will as soon as you get your lips over here and kiss me, doll." He leaned over the bar. She did the same and kissed him. Hoots and hollers started, and she quickly stepped back.

"That should do it," Jeb said with his arms crossed in front of his chest, appearing pissed off.

"What's wrong?" she asked him.

"When do you get off?" he snapped at her.

She pulled her bottom lip between her teeth and looked at the others. Jaxon seemed even angrier.

"It's only eleven. I close up, remember?"

"Let's get comfortable, men. It's going to be a long night," Gator stated, and they ordered some beers.

Alana poured them and felt a bit annoyed. Were they going to stay here and scare off all the patrons who flirted with her? How was she going to make any tips?

She decided to ignore them as their friends joined them and they seemed to let down their aggressive guard. Alana walked down to the end of the bar and saw the man by the corner. He waved her over, and she noticed the way he kept a hand on the bar and played with a die. He moved one in between his fingers smoothly and without even looking down. As she approached, she recognized him as that guy she'd seen at the fair. The one who she'd apparently helped in the clothing store. He smiled at her.

"So I figured out where the second place was that I saw you before. Casper's. How are you, Alana?"

She felt a bit uneasy that the guy knew her name and she didn't know his. She needed a reprieve from Geno and the guys so she placed a coaster onto the bar and smiled.

"You have me at a disadvantage. You know my name, but I don't know yours."

"Just call me Neil." He reached out to shake her hand, and she did. He gave it a squeeze, and she felt nothing, but he held her gaze and looked her over.

"What can I get for you?"

"A martini. Dry and shaken, not stirred."

She gave him a nod and then prepared the drink in front of him. He continued to roll the die between his fingers, and she poured the martini into the glass.

"Olive?"

"Two, please." She added them.

"What's with the die? That's pretty cool."

"Oh, just an old habit. I used to enjoy the casinos, but now I kind of just like the roll of the dice and where it may lead me, or to whom."

She knew he was flirting, but just barely. She was going to respond, but someone asked her for a drink, and when she looked at Neil, he seemed angry for someone interrupting her. There was something about this guy, yet he seemed so nice.

The bar got busier as the night went on. Neil left after a little while, and her men disappeared to a side table.

It had slowed down a bit, and she checked her cell phone and looked up her e-mails. When she scrolled down and saw the one from Gabe's parents, Mike and Marcy, she felt sick to her stomach. They were still suffering, and here she knew Gabe was alive and well and his parents, and the community in Scrantonville, didn't. It wasn't right, and she would have to talk to Gabe. He had to come clean and, at a minimum, call his parents.

* * * *

"No! No!" He roared in anger and slammed his hands down on the steering wheel as he watched the men walk his woman to her car. She wasn't driving. One of them took her keys but not before kissing her and running his hands along her hips and ass. Another pulled her into his arms then pressed her against the car like some whore. He felt as if he was going to break a blood vessel in his eye as he watched in horror as five men took her with them. She was fucking five men.

"Fuck!"

He watched them leave, and his mind scattered with crazy thoughts. What should he do next? How would he make her suffer for what she'd done? He was committed to her. He'd practiced on those other two women so he could get it right. Now he needed to change things. He would need to cleanse her of her sins. Wash away their stench, their touch, from her body.

He needed something. He needed to make a plan. He needed to work through this anger, this fury, and then straighten out his mind and take her. The time was drawing closer. He should be with Alana tonight, not them. Five fucking men.

"Five fucking men. You're mine. Mine!" he yelled as he watched the headlights of her car and their truck disappear out of the parking lot. He looked around him. Heart racing, head pounding, he locked onto her. She stumbled slightly.

A blonde, not a brunette like Alana, but a similar figure. He looked around. She was all alone. He smirked as she came closer and fumbled with her keys. She was parked right next to him. He rolled down the window and calmed his excitement.

"Honey, I don't think you should be driving."

"I'm okay." She lowered down to lean against the open window. Her blouse parted, and her breasts flowed from some shimmering camisole she wore. She pulled her bottom lip between her teeth and gazed at him. He knew he was attractive. That got them every time.

"I can give you a ride, honey. You really shouldn't drink and drive."

"I don't know you though." She twirled her blonde hair between her fingers.

"What's to know? I'm a nice guy offering a pretty woman a ride home so she doesn't kill herself," he said and smirked. He would be the one doing the killing.

"Well, I should just go back inside and let my friend know."

"The friend who let you leave Casper's drunk so you could drive?" he challenged her and raised one of his eyebrows at her.

She squinted her eyes, swayed a little, and then pulled open the door. "You're right. Screw that bitch. She took a hot guy right out of my grasp tonight. I was flirting with him all night." She slid into the front seat then closed the door. Her skirt lifted higher, and she didn't even notice. He looked her over. She would do just fine.

"Where do you live?"

"Outside of town."

"Roommate?"

"In there and not planning on coming home tonight."

He placed the car in drive and slowly pulled out of the parking lot.

"What's your name, sweetheart?" he asked her.

"Jenny."

"Well, Jenny, I'm Neil. Tell me, do you think we have control over our destinies, or are they out of our hands?"

She looked at him, and then smiled softly.

"Oh, I believe our destiny is already written in stone."

"Interesting. Maybe we'll find out if that's true tonight or not."

He looked straight ahead and planned his game. Perhaps tonight wasn't a waste after all. He would prove to Jenny that he had the power to control destiny. He held her life in his hands.

Chapter 7

When Alana got out of the shower, Geno was there to greet her. He licked his lips before he wrapped her in a towel and helped to dry her off.

"Feel better?" he asked her.

"Yes, and you?" she challenged him.

Geno knew he'd acted angry and jealous all night and that Alana had picked up on it. But he was new to being in a committed relationship and feeling so close and attached to Alana.

He gripped her hips and held her in place.

"I was fine. I'm fine now."

"You were being a jerk before." She stepped from his hold and walked closer to the counter. She ran her fingers through her hair and then held his gaze through the reflection in the mirror.

"I don't like other men flirting with you and suggesting you go to the local motel with them to fuck," he snapped at her.

She turned around. Her towel loosened, and she held it against her chest. It barely covered her breasts and exposed both of her thighs. His mouth watered, and his dick hardened.

"Geno, I never fucked every guy who suggested it to me. Why would I do that now?"

He couldn't believe her attitude. He deserved it. She was right. But it still pissed him off that guys would actually suggest it.

He stepped into her space but didn't touch her. He could feel the power between them, the lust, the desire, and it wouldn't be long before he had his dick deep into her pussy, claiming her and easing his anger and fears.

"I don't like it, okay? I don't like other men wanting what's mine and my team's."

She took a deep breath then released it, as if she were contemplating his words.

Then she reached up and cupped his cheek. She had to stand up on tiptoes to reach him, and she still was only tall enough to kiss his chin and lower lip.

"None of them matter but you, Jeb, Jaxon, Gator, and Gabe. None of them."

He lifted her up into his arms, and she straddled his waist.

"I'm new at this whole commitment thing, and at having such strong feelings for a woman. I can't promise that I won't blow my stack or get jealous. I can't promise that I won't need to fuck you so damn hard and deeply that you only have me and the feel of my cock deep inside of your pussy imbedded in your head."

"Oh God, Geno. I love when you're deep inside of me. I need you all the time. I need all of you."

He thrust his hips as he smiled.

"That's exactly what I need right now."

He carried her out of the bathroom and entered the bedroom. Jaxon was lying on the edge of the bed, stroking his cock, and Jeb was undressing.

"We thought we heard something about Alana's pussy," Jeb said, and Alana gasped then laid her face against Geno's chest, embarrassed by Jeb's words.

"We heard that too," Gator said. He and Gabe sat on two chairs, just watching.

"Well, there you go. Jaxon, get our woman ready for cock. We're going to fill her up and make her see that she's our woman and no one else can ever have her."

"With pleasure," Jaxon said as Geno handed her over to him. Jaxon lifted her up and over him so her pussy was over his face.

He gripped her hips, and Alana moaned aloud as she tried grabbing onto his shoulders. Jaxon hummed and ate at her cream while Geno got undressed.

Jeb handed Geno the lube as Jaxon fingered Alana and sucked on her pussy. They were all feeling aroused and needy. They had worried about her as guys hit on her at Casper's but also as they heard the news about a second young woman being abducted, tortured, and killed. None of them wanted Alana out of his sight.

Jeb climbed onto the bed as Jaxon lowered Alana over his shaft. She gripped his cock and sank down onto Jaxon as he cupped her breasts.

"Fuck, that pussy is hot and warm. You feel like heaven, doll. Absolute heaven."

Alana rocked her hips and rode Jaxon as he manipulated her breasts. Jeb gently ran his fingers through her hair, gripped her hair and head, and then covered her mouth and kissed her. She continued to rock her hips and jerked a moment as Geno prepared her ass for his taking.

Jeb released her lips and smiled at her.

"I've got something for you." He stroked his cock, and she licked her lips just as Geno tapped her ass.

"I've got something for her too."

Jeb glanced to the left and watched Geno press lube to Alana's ass. She continued to slowly rock over Jaxon and then gasped as Jaxon pinched her nipples.

"Suck Jeb's cock. Work him good while the three of us take you together. Always together, Alana. Always all of us and you," Jaxon said, and she nodded then moved her mouth toward Jeb's cock.

* * * *

Jeb held her head, feeling aroused by the control. It also seemed to turn Alana on. She really was very submissive.

The moment her mouth moved over Jeb's cock, he closed his eyes and went still. He wanted to thrust into her sexy mouth so badly, but he didn't want to hurt her or overwhelm her. When she was ready for him to move faster, she would let him know.

"Aw, honey, I thought about this ass all night. Watching you walk back and forth behind the bar, then bend over to get things... So badly I would have loved to join you back behind that bar and fuck you so every fucking guy in the place would know who you belong to," Geno confessed, and Jeb felt his cock grow harder and thicker.

She moaned against Jeb's cock.

"I think she's turned on by that idea, Geno," Jeb said and ran the palm of his hand over her ass as Geno spread her ass cheeks and aligned his cock with her puckered hole.

"Is that right, baby? You want my cock in your ass?"

She moaned and nodded her head. Geno chuckled, and Jeb gripped her hair a little tighter and moved his hips a little faster. Jaxon gripped her hips and held himself still with his cock in her pussy as Geno began to push into her anus, filling her with cock.

In a flash they were all moving. Alana was sucking Jeb's cock harder and faster as he began to rock into her mouth. Geno was thrusting in counter thrusts to Jaxon's strokes, and Alana was moaning and shaking as she orgasmed again and again.

"You're ours, Alana. All ours," Geno said and thrust into her faster.

"Fuck I'm coming. Fuck, baby, your mouth is incredible." Jeb held himself still and came, shooting his load down her throat and shivering as Alana suckled and licked him clean.

Jeb fell back to the bed, and Alana screamed with another release as Jaxon came and then Geno followed, shaking and roaring like a wild man.

* * * *

Gator watched as Geno pulled from Alana's ass, and he took his place, wrapping his arm around her midsection and holding her upright. Jaxon pinched her nipples and smiled as he rolled out of the way. Gator pressed her down to the bed on her belly and thrust into her pussy from behind. She gripped the comforter, and he lifted her hips higher, thrusting and stroking her as she thrust back.

"That's it, baby. You were made for us. For me." He continued to rock into her. He felt the tap to his shoulder, and there was Gabe. He held a tube of lube in his hand and tapped it on his palm as he raised one of his eyebrows up and down. Gator smiled and winked. Gabe wanted to make love to Alana too, and he was going to try to take her ass from behind, despite his injuries.

Gator pulled from her pussy, and Alana moaned in protest.

"Gabe is joining us, Alana," he told her, and she looked over her shoulder.

Her eyes glued on to Gabe and then down to the tube of lube he tapped in the palm of his hand. She bit her lower lip and then let Gator move underneath her. She straddled Gator's hips and sank right down onto his cock.

Gator smiled up at her and gave her a wink. He could see her concern, and he jerked his hips harder upward, forcing her focus back on him and to not be concerned and worry. She got the message and closed her eyes and rode Gator's cock.

* * * *

Gabe was nervous that he wouldn't be able to take Alana like this. His legs were weak from the injuries, but he wanted to make love to her and share her equally. They all got to fuck her ass and find pleasure and satisfaction in knowing they were the only ones to ever take her that way. He wanted that too. Especially after tonight and feeling the same insecurities and jealousy his team members were.

Gabe caressed her ass cheeks and then squeezed some lube into her ass.

"Damn, baby, you want this badly, don't you?" he asked her and then pressed a finger to her hole and worked the lube in there. She thrust her ass back and moaned.

"Yes, Gabe. Please take me. I need you inside too. I'm going to come."

He gripped her hips and stopped moving his finger in her ass.

"Don't you dare come. You come when I tell you."

"Oh God."

"Do you understand?" he asked firmly.

"Yes. Yes, Gabe, whatever you say. Whatever you want. Just take me."

He pulled his fingers from her ass and shook with anticipation. His legs were shaking, but he wanted Alana this way so badly his cock ached with need.

He slowly aligned his cock with her puckered hole and spread her ass cheeks.

"Nice and easy, baby. Here I come." He began to push into her ass and felt his legs shaking. He begged his body to hold on and allow him to take her like this. To make love to her with Gator and fill her with cock, claiming her as theirs.

As he eased in, he felt the pain, and then he paused.

"Please, Gabe. Do it. Stop teasing me."

She thought he was teasing her, but really, he was weak, his legs and the damn injuries too much to stay upright like this.

"Take her, Gabe," Jaxon ordered.

"Fuck that ass, Gabe," Geno told him.

Gabe pushed deeper, and the sensations, the tightness, and warmth against his cock felt like a vise grip. "Holy fuck, you're so tight. Damn, baby, let me in."

"Relax, Alana. He's fine. Let him in," Gator told her.

Gabe felt her widen her thighs and released a long sigh. Gabe pushed deeper and sank all the way in.

"Holy fuck," he said as he held her ass.

"Move, Gabe. I'm not going to last much longer," Gator stated, and Gabe began to move. He focused on the feel of taking Alana like this. Of her being so trusting and giving of herself to let them fuck her in every hole.

He was panting, his brow wet with perspiration as he increased his speed.

"Yes. Yes, Gabe, harder, fuck me harder."

Alana screamed, and he and Gator took control. They thrust and stroked into her, making her moan and beg for more. His legs felt numb, and he could hardly catch his breath as he slammed into her ass and came just as Alana and Gator did.

He fell against her then felt the hands on his arms. Jaxon was there to help him sit down.

He eased out of her ass and stumbled to the side of the bed

He caught sight of Jaxon walking away but not before he gave Alana's ass a smack.

Gabe was overwhelmed with emotion. They were more than buddies, soldiers of a team. They were brothers. They were family, and because of Alana, they were bound for life, and nothing could ever destroy what they shared. Nothing.

* * * *

Alana was looking at her phone and re-reading the e-mail from Michael and Marcy.

She couldn't even reply. How could she? Whatever she said was laced with lies.

All is well. I'm doing fine. Just working two jobs and getting involved in a ménage relationship with five Marines. Oh, and one of them is Gabe. He's alive, by the way.

Shit.

She screeched as she felt the hand on her shoulder. She turned to find Gabe there.

"Hey, what's wrong?" he asked, drawing attention from Jaxon, who was looking at the computer screen and appearing serious with his eyes squinted and concern on his face.

"Just reading e-mails."

"From who?" he asked as he sat down on the couch next to her and placed his arm over her shoulders.

She pulled her bottom lip between her teeth.

"From your parents."

Gabe pulled back, and Jaxon looked up from the laptop.

She tried to gauge Gabe's reaction, and he looked away from her toward the window that looked out over the backyard.

Alana covered his arm.

"You need to tell them you're alive."

He stood up and limped toward the window, using his cane for support.

"Gabe?"

"Alana, I can't. I'm not ready for that."

She stood up and walked toward him.

"Gabe, they're so sad. They miss you so much, and this isn't right. I get to love you, to hold you in my arms and be with you, but your parents still think you're dead. You have to let them know. You have to let everyone know that you're alive."

"Jesus, baby." He ran his hand over his mouth and turned toward the window.

Alana wrapped her arms around his waist from behind and pressed her head and cheek against his back.

"So many people love you Gabe. Let the fear, the insecurities go. You're not a failure. You're a hero, and I love you."

Gabe turned around and hugged her. She placed her cheek against his chest and looked at Jaxon, Geno, Gator, and Jeb.

"It's your choice, Gabe. We'll be there right by your side the entire time," Gator told him.

"I'll need all of you," Gabe said.

"Looks like we're heading to Scrantonville," Jaxon said, and Alana smiled.

Chapter 8

Gabe was a nervous wreck as they all drove out early Sunday morning to Scrantonville. Alana called into work to say she wouldn't be there for a few days. Jaxon had suggested that they call Gabe's parents and let them know he was coming. Alana had informed them that Gabe's grandparents were still alive and elderly, and the shock could upset them if they just showed up at the front door.

But he was still freaking out, worrying that everyone would hate him, see him as a failure and an invalid, and he started to have second thoughts.

But as they rolled into town, Alana holding his hand, texting to someone then smiling at him reassuringly, and his brothers surrounding him, he couldn't believe the sight.

A large banner hung from one side of the entrance gates to town to the other, saying, "Welcome Home, Gabe—Scrantonville's Own Hero."

Jaxon pulled the truck into the one open spot left for them, and the music and cheering grew louder.

The local high school band was there, playing the second the truck pulled up, and all he could see was the sea of people cheering, holding up signs.

They all got out of the truck. He walked with his cane, Alana and his brothers by his sides as his eyes filled with tears.

He turned to look at Alana, feeling overwhelmed and at a loss.

"Did you plan this? Did you put them up to this?" he asked in disbelief. An expression of insult and shock crossed her face before tears filled her eyes. She shook her head.

"You see, Gabe? You are a hero, and everyone in Scrantonville knows it. You've touched people's lives, and when that happens, it's special, just like you."

He shook his head as his eyes welled up with tears. He hugged her, and then he heard his mother's voice.

Marcy and Michael ran forward and stopped in front of him. His mother was hysterically crying, her hand over her mouth, staring at him in disbelief. His father had his arm wrapped around her shoulder, and he, too, had tears rolling down his cheeks.

"Gabe," his father said.

"Don't cry, Mom. I'm here, and I'm alive."

They hugged him tight as they cried about miracles and having their son return home to them safe and sound.

This was the second best day of his life. The first one was when Alana had shown up in Tranquility and forced him to realize she still loved him and that he wasn't a failure in her eyes. The second was this moment. To feel his mother's hug and the healing it provided him just like when he was a child and got hurt. All the pain and fear disappeared. It was magical. He was a grown man with so many misconceptions and fears holding him back. He could have lost the opportunity to feel the power of his mother's and father's embrace, as well as the love and embrace of the people in the community he grew up in. He owed it all to Alana, the love of his life, his heart and his soul, his everything.

* * * *

Neil stood in the woods and hid within the trees. He peered through the binoculars and watched the house for several hours. No movement and no sign of Alana. She hadn't been at work the last several days, and he needed to see her. His quick fix turned out to be more than he had anticipated, and when he'd killed her, he had left a trail of blood behind him.

Her roommate arrived home after all, and she wasn't alone.

He had barely gotten his clothes on. He was certain he'd forgotten something and had left something behind. He had to make his move. He needed to grab Alana and take her away someplace they could be alone. He was going to keep her forever.

He knew his truck was stocked with everything he needed. Guns, food, ammunition, clothes, and even things for Alana to wear. Although he loved her in skirts and in all her classy dresses, it didn't make sense for her to wear such things where they were going. He leaned against the tree and wondered where she could be. He tried to fight the thought that she was with them. Four assholes and one invalid. The fucking soldiers were weak and useless. He was the real deal. He'd killed so many fucking people that the government discharged him. He'd been making progress and kicking ass like a Marine should do. Those damn pussies in the government wanted to sit behind a desk all cushy and comfy while soldiers died left and right for bureaucratic bullshit. Not him. He wasn't going to die in the middle of some fucking desert within some godforsaken village of terrorist assholes and their families. He'd done what he had to do, and the government, his own leaders, found fault in that.

Fuck them, and fuck those five pussies who are trying to take my woman away from me.

He pointed his rifle at the house and used the sight to clearly mark the back doorway.

"If one of you fuckheads are standing there, and in the way of me getting my woman, I'm going to blow your fucking head off."

He pretended to pull the trigger and pretended to make the sound of a shot.

He chuckled and lowered his weapon. "I've always been a patient man, and I always take a direct order and follow that order until the mission is complete."

He looked to his side.

"Isn't that right, commander?"

He smirked to himself. He'd prove he was the best soldier ever, even to his dead commander and the rest of his troop who could no longer join the fight with him.

* * * *

"You're something else, do you know that?" Jeb asked Alana as he wrapped his arms around her waist and held her from behind.

She stared out toward the barbecue and all Gabe's family and friends.

"Me? I didn't do anything," she whispered.

He kissed her neck and inhaled against her skin.

"Doll, you brought him back to us, to his family and to you."

She turned in his arms and ran her hands up his chest to his shoulders, her expression serious.

"What do you mean?" she asked.

Jeb looked over her shoulder and saw Gabe smiling and talking with some friends. Jaxon, Gator, and Geno were laughing with Gabe's mom and dad, and Jeb felt content.

"Gabe had so many issues when he retired from the Corps. A lot of guys lose their minds or try to hurt themselves. He just closed up and wouldn't allow anyone in. We all had a rough time. Nightmares, anxiety attacks, and just trying to fit in. But Gabe shut down. He was abrupt and angry all the time, and he wanted nothing to do with talking about his home or his past. Jaxon even tried to encourage him to call his family. We didn't even know about you."

She looked down, and he lifted her chin back up with his fingers.

"Hey, I'm not kidding when I say he was fucked up."

"I know. He was pretty straightforward about wanting me to think of him as dead," she said.

"But you changed that. You changed all of us. You really brought this team together like we haven't been in years. I mean we've always relied on one another and just knew we needed to continue to live our lives as a team, but we never expected to feel the way you've made us feel, Alana. You truly complete us, and I want you to know that I love you."

"Oh, Jeb, I love you too." She stood up on tiptoes, and he lifted her higher so he could kiss her.

"Hey, if she's handing out kisses, I want some too," Gator teased, joining them.

Jeb released her to Gator, who pulled her into his arms and hugged her.

"You're an angel, doll, our very own angel, and I love you," he told her.

"And I love you."

"And what about me?" Geno asked.

She chuckled, and Jeb smiled wide.

"Who couldn't love you?" she said, pulling him closer by his shirt. She stood up on tiptoes and whispered to him, "And that dirty little mouth and mind of yours." She kissed him.

Geno ran his hands along her ass, squeezing her.

"You're the one who mentioned getting dirty. I've got some very dirty thoughts about you and this fine piece of ass."

She gave his shoulder a smack, and Jeb laughed.

* * * *

Jaxon was standing by the large tree and swing where Jim and Teddy were. They talked about the recent murders of two young women and how they were trying to catch the guy.

'Yeah, I read about it in the papers and online. Sick bastard. Are you guys any closer to catching him?"

"Gunner has some leads. That's why we can't stay long. We have to get back to Salvation," Teddy told him.

"Yeah, it's a terrible situation. People are beginning to panic," Jim said.

"Well, maybe it will make women more aware of what's going on around them and remind them not to take chances. You know, follow their instincts," Jaxon said as he looked over at Alana with his team. She was young, sexy, and beautiful, just as the two women who were killed had been. It made his stomach ache and his gut clench with concern.

He didn't know why he felt so worried.

"Do you think this guy knew the women or just randomly chose them?" he asked.

"I think randomly chose them. Opportunity of convenience. Hopefully he'll screw up soon, and we'll catch him."

Jaxon watched Alana as she walked down from the porch and some guys, who were friends of hers, stopped her. They hugged her, and she smiled as she kissed them back but quickly pulled away. He supposed he would always have this protective feeling over her. She was such a sweet woman with a great big heart, and people instantly liked her. In a matter of weeks, she had changed their lives. He knew what his job was and what it would continue to be. To protect Alana and his team. No matter what the cost, he would always put them first and do what was best for them. Nothing would change that.

* * * *

Gabe clasped her hands above her head as he thrust his hips. Alana's legs hung over his thighs and against his waist as he thrust his cock deep, up into her pussy.

She held his gaze, and he absorbed every ounce of love and passion combusting between them. The way her large breasts bounced with each stroke of his cock. How her long brown hair cascaded over the pillows and how her chest heaved up and down.

"I love you, baby. I love being inside of you."

"I love you too," she said, and he lowered down and held himself, still not wanting to come. Not until the others joined them.

He glanced to the right, and there stood Jaxon. He stroked his cock and stared at Alana.

Gabe lowered down and used all his strength to roll her to the right so she was now straddling him.

Jaxon reached out and ran his palms along her ass cheeks.

"Baby, I've waited three days to have you, and it was fucking torture."

She smiled as she thrust up and down, riding Gabe. Gabe reached up and cupped her breasts. She moaned and jerked a moment, and Gabe knew that Jaxon was stimulating her.

"Where do you want my cock, Alana?" Jaxon asked.

"Oh, Jaxon, please. Don't tease me."

Geno approached, ran his fingers through her hair, and gripped her head. She looked up toward him.

"Tell him, baby. We all want to hear that sweet little mouth talk dirty. Then, if you're a good girl, I'm going to fuck this mouth. You want that?"

"Yes. Yes, Geno."

Jeb joined in. "Then tell him."

"Tell me where you want my cock," Jaxon pushed.

"My ass. Fuck my ass, Jaxon, please."

"Hot damn, you don't need to ask me twice," Jaxon said.

Gabe lifted her up then lowered her back down on his shaft. He watched Gabe pull her toward him and then saw Alana open her mouth and begin to lick and taste Geno's cock. She moaned loudly, and he felt the pressure, heard Jaxon moan, and then he knew Jaxon had penetrated her ass fully. That was it. They all lost it and began to thrust, stroke, and rock, making the bed shake as they filled Alana in every hole.

"Fuck, I'm there. Damn, baby," Gabe said as he came inside of her.

Geno followed after and fell to the bed. Jaxon was still thrusting into her ass.

* * * *

Gator watched, and he looked at Jeb, and then they both joined in. Jaxon lifted her up and back, keeping his dick in her ass as he gave orders.

Gabe moved out of the way, and so did Geno.

Jeb and Gator knelt on the bed and watched Alana as they stroked their cocks.

"Spread your thighs. Use your fingers to open your pussy lips while I fuck this ass."

"Jaxon. Oh God, Jaxon." She moaned and slightly fell forward as she came.

"Holy shit, that is hot. Damn, she likes you ordering her around, Jaxon. You should see her cream dripping from her pussy," Jeb said, and he stroked a finger over her pussy then pressed up into her.

She moaned and thrust as Gator licked her nipple and pulled on it. He swirled his tongue around her breast then tugged.

"I think Jeb needs to feel your mouth on him, baby. Open that mouth and suck his cock," Jaxon ordered then lowered her down so she could reach Jeb. Jeb held his cock in his hand as he leaned back on his heels on the bed. Alana's thighs were spread wide, and Jaxon was slowly moving in and out of her ass.

Gator was staring at her, and Jaxon knew he wanted some too.

Alana sucked Jeb's cock until Jaxon gave her ass a smack.

"Now, Gator," he ordered.

She released Jeb's cock and moved her head to the right toward Gator. Gator grabbed her hair and head as she opened wide and took him inside of her mouth.

"Fuck, that is hot. Damn, baby, I'm going to come."

Jaxon rocked his hips, and Alana pulled from Gator's cock.

Jeb continued to play with her pussy, pushing his finger in and out of her cunt as Gator nipped her nipple.

"Stop teasing me and fuck me already," she yelled, and Jaxon stopped. Gator, Jeb, Gabe, and Geno all looked at her. Geno whistled.

"Damn, Jaxon, she told you."

Alana screamed as Jaxon pulled from her ass, flipped her over his lap, and smacked her ass.

"Jaxon!" she yelled as she held onto his leg so she wouldn't fall, and Jaxon gave a series of smacks to her ass.

* * * *

Alana's heart was pounding in her chest, and once the dizziness subsided, she yelled out again.

"Oh. Oh!" she moaned.

"Hot damn, I love this woman," Gator said and ran his palms up her thighs, spreading them as Jaxon spanked her ass.

She felt Gator's fingers press up into her pussy as someone spread her thighs wider, making one leg drop off of Jaxon's lap.

She found herself rocking and thrusting against Jaxon as he randomly smacked her ass in between Gator's strokes with his finger in her pussy.

"Please, Jaxon. Please, I can't take it," she begged.

Jaxon chuckled, and Gator pulled his fingers from her cunt.

"Get on the bed, Gator," Jaxon ordered as he turned her around and placed her on top of Gator.

Alana held his gaze. His blue eyes sparkled with desire and hunger as she sank down onto his shaft. She felt so wet and slick that she could hear the sounds as their bodies collided. Jaxon pushed her down gently, and then she felt the cool, liquid to her anus again, and the anticipation was killing her.

"Please. Please, Jaxon," she begged, actually begged to be fucked in the ass by Jaxon.

She felt the fingers in her hair and then her head being turned to the right. There was Jeb with his cock in his hand, waiting for her to suck him.

"Now," Jeb ordered.

She gulped, her heart pounded, and she opened wide and took him into her mouth. Behind her, Jaxon stroked into her ass in one smooth thrust, filling her. That was it. She lost focus as her body tightened like a bow about to break and she came. Jaxon and Gator rocked into her hard and fast. Jeb held her head and stroked faster into her mouth. Suddenly the three of them roared, and they came at once, filling her with their seed and marking her, ruining her for anyone but her five lusty lovers. She was exhausted as her eyes closed, and nothing else mattered but relishing the aftermath of their night of pleasure.

Chapter 9

Alana was working at the boutique in the back room when her cell phone rang. She saw the caller ID as she placed the last set of sweaters onto the rack that needed to be wheeled out front by Monique. It was Jaxon.

"Where are you?" he demanded to know.

"Jaxon, where do you think I am?" she asked, chuckling.

"Shit. Sorry. How is everything going? Will she need you much longer?"

"I know it's a Sunday, but with the winter clothing line coming in, and people already shopping for the holidays, we're behind. I think I'll be at least a few more hours."

"Damn. We're meeting at Casper's."

"I can meet you there when I'm done."

"No. One of us will come get you."

"I can get a ride with Monique. It's not a big deal. What's wrong with you? Something is up."

He sighed on the line and then exhaled.

"You heard about the young woman that went missing last weekend?"

"Yes, of course."

"Well, she was at Casper's that night. Her friend thought she had left with someone, and then when she got to their place, the killer was there. They found her body and some evidence. They think the guy might be in Tranquility."

"Oh God, that's terrible. Did her friend walk in on it?"

"Not really sure. Gunner isn't saying much except that they have some concrete evidence. The killer screwed up and left clues behind and fingerprints. They'll hopefully have him identified soon."

"Well, that's good news then."

"Not until he's caught and behind bars. I want you to call me when you and Monique are done. One of us will come pick you ladies up."

"Okay, Jaxon. I'd better go, or it will be four hours more instead of three."

"Watch it, you."

"Or else what, exactly?" she teased, knowing he was such a control freak.

"You know exactly what. A nice pink ass."

"Hmm. Promises, promises."

"Later, doll."

"Later, Marine."

Alana disconnected the call and chuckled.

She didn't know where Monique had disappeared to as she stood up and started pushing the rack of sweaters out to the front. They had a display prepared, and Mrs. Hamlet wanted things done perfectly.

As she pushed the cart to the dark room, she wondered why all the lights were off. She knew that Mrs. Hamlet wanted her customers surprised by the new displays, but how could they even see what they were doing?

"Monique? Mrs. Hamlet?" She stopped the cart in front of the empty display. She thought she heard something and turned around. There was someone standing there.

She gasped and then heard the voice.

"Hello, Alana. I've been waiting for you."

She recognized the voice, and then he came out of the shadows.

"Neil?" She looked around her, not really processing what was happening here. His eyes seemed to widen that she'd remembered his name, and in a series of quick, panicked thoughts, she wondered if he was some lunatic.

He was on her in a flash, and she turned to run, but he grabbed her arm. His hold was forceful and firm. His tight grip scared her, and she tried pulling away and demanding he release her.

"Let me go. Let me go," she yelled at him, and when the smack came out of nowhere, her head snapped back, and she reacted. She used her left fist, her weak arm, to throw a punch at him. He slapped her forearm down hard, making her bone burn and tears fill her eyes.

Then he slapped her again.

She was going to fight when he gripped her throat and demanded she cooperate.

"Stop fighting me. We don't have the time for this. Those two bitches will wake up soon enough, and then the cops will come. Let's move now."

"I'm not going anywhere with you."

He released his hold on her throat and pulled out a gun. A Beretta.

He pointed to the right, and that was when she saw Monique and Mrs. Hamlet tied up to the display and unconscious. Both were bleeding from their lips.

She gasped, and he stared at her, still holding Alana's arm but his gun pointed at Monique.

"I'll kill them both right now if you don't come with me. I'll shoot them right in the head, and you'll have to live with that."

The tears stung her eyes. She was scared.

"Why are you doing this?"

He brought the gun closer to her. He placed the barrel under her chin and then let it slide between her breasts, parting her blouse.

"Because you're mine, and I've waited for you for far too long."

He turned her around, making her scream as he forced her from the main room to the back room. He shoved the back door open, and she knew that would signal the silent alarm. Perhaps he wasn't so prepared after all.

Alana needed to buy herself some time. She had to stall him or God knows what he might do to her. If he was the one who killed those other women, then she was as good as dead.

* * * *

"So what else do you have on this guy? Any description?" Gabe asked Kenny.

Teddy, Jim, Gunner, and a few officers were walking around the bar and restaurant at Casper's, asking if anyone had remembered seeing the young woman talking with a man. It was obvious that she'd left here with him, but they weren't sure if they'd met inside or outside. Her car never left the parking lot.

"Not much really. We found some die at the crime scene, not sure if it was the killers or what.

"Die?" he asked.

"Yeah." Gabe looked at Gator.

"Do you remember that night a couple of weeks ago we came in here and those guys were hitting on Alana?"

"Yeah, we got rid of them."

"Well, later on, some guy was at the end of the bar talking to Alana. He was playing with die, rolling it between his fingers."

"Really?" Jim asked as his cell phone rang.

Jaxon started asking Gabe about the man and the dice.

Jim stood up and locked gazes with Gunner.

"What's going on?"

"We got a name, fingerprints, and a suspect. He lives in Tranquility."

"What does he look like? Who is he?" Gabe asked as Gunner walked over.

Jaxon explained what Gabe had shared about the man with the die.

"Hold that thought," Gunner said and then pulled up an e-mail on his phone.

"Did he look like this guy?" Gunner asked.

Geno and Gator looked at it.

"That's him," Geno said.

"Oh shit, Alana," Gabe said just as Gunner's phone rang and Kenny and Jim's radio's went off.

"There's a disturbance at the boutique. The silent alarm went off by the back door," Gunner told them.

"Alana. Oh shit, he could be trying to take Alana," Gabe shouted.

"Let's move," Jaxon yelled, and they all hurried out to their trucks. Gabe was scared out of his mind.

"I never should have allowed her to go there tonight. It's not even her regular shift," Jaxon carried on as he hopped into his truck. Gunner, Jim, and Kenny were already squealing out of the parking lot, lights flashing and heading into Tranquility.

"I hope we're not too late. God, let us get to her in time," Jeb said, and they drove in silence as each of them tried to call and text her.

* * * *

Alana struggled to get free. Neil had been so busy tying her hands up that he hadn't even seen her cell phone. His focus was on her breasts, and she knew she needed to keep him from seeing her cell. As he drove out of town, she heard the sirens and could hear the police cars passing by them. She had been right. The silent alarm had gone off.

She needed to get her phone on and call the guys before the signal was lost.

"Why are you doing this? Where are you taking me?" she asked as she moved her hands to her back pocket and tried to remember what buttons to press to get a call out.

She thought she heard a deep voice and panicked, thinking that it was one of the guys, and they were yelling to her through the phone. If she didn't cover that up, then Neil would know she'd made the call. He looked at her, and she knew she must have looked crazy with fear.

"I don't know why you're doing this, Neil. What did I ever do to you?" she asked and turned so that her body was against the side door.

"I chose you, Alana. You and I are meant for one another. I told you this before."

"When?"

"At the fair when I bumped into you. Now stop asking me fucking questions. I need to concentrate. We have to get to the cabin."

"What cabin? Where?"

"Shut the fuck up. You'll know where when we get there."

"I don't want to go. Just stop this blue truck and let me out right now on Highway 10," she said.

"No," he yelled, and then he looked at her. He let his eyes roam over her body, and suddenly he pulled over, making her lose her balance. She fell against the dashboard. He reached for her back pocket.

"You stupid fucking bitch! You think those Marines and those loser cops can help you? You're never going to see them again. I'm your Marine now, and as soon as I get you to the cabin, I'm going to cleanse you of their stench and make you mine. Fuck you!" he yelled into the phone and then threw it out the window.

Alana cried as he then smacked her in the back of the head, making her face hit the dashboard. "Stop hitting me please."

"You'll pay for that. Soon enough."

* * * *

"Fuck!" Jaxon yelled out as they all listened in on the phone call. Gunner was on speaker, listening as best he could.

"We can't be far behind them," Gunner said. "She gave a description of the truck, the color, and the road they were on. Kenny called it in. Let's keep in that direction but keep your distance. This guy killed three women. We're not taking any chances with Alana."

They headed that way, but an hour later, it was as if the truck, Alana, and Neil had disappeared. The guys were on the side of the road next to a huge area of woods and hunting land as Gunner spoke on his cell phone and other cops gathered around them.

"It's getting dark. She must be so scared," Gabe said as he leaned against the truck.

"I'm going to kill him. When I get my hands on him, he's going to die," Jaxon said as he ran his hand over his mouth and thought about all the terrible things Neil could be doing to her.

"He mentioned a cabin in the woods. Have you looked into any cabins nearby here? Anything we could start searching?" Gator asked.

"It's getting dark out. The chopper is still looking around nearby. Anything is possible, but they can't see in the dark. It would be like trying to find a needle in a haystack. They're burning light," Kenny said. His cell phone rang.

"It's Deanna. Let me take this. She's a mess right now."

Jaxon looked at his team. "I can't stand sitting here and doing nothing. He's going to kill her," Jaxon said.

"We can't think like that. Alana is smart. Look at the description of the truck and location she gave. Look how she hid her phone and used it to call you," Gator said to him.

"The chopper found something," Gunner said and waved them over.

"What did they find?" Jaxon asked, and Gunner listened in.

"We got a location on a cabin and a truck like Alana described parked inside of an outdoor garage. They almost missed it, but the doors to the garage are off."

They listened and waited for Gunner to get more details and organize a plan.

"Whatever the plan is, we're part of it. We're going in. She's our woman, our responsibility, and we failed her. That isn't going to happen again," Jaxon said.

Gunner nodded as chaos erupted around them as they planned to infiltrate the cabin in the woods and save Alana.

* * * *

Alana fell to the floor again. His strikes to her skin were painful, and she was beginning to lose hope that help was coming.

He was completely insane as he spoke to some imaginary commander about completing a mission and being free once and for all. She tried to talk to him and calm him down, but he raged on about cleansing her as he stripped her blouse off of her.

Her hands were tied in front of her, and he used them to drag her around the room then punish her for sleeping with her five men.

Alana's lips were bloody, her eyes sore and swollen nearly shut, but she wasn't going to give in to this psycho. She was the daughter of a Marine, and if she was going to die, then she was going to die fighting to the very end.

"Is this what you do? Does this make you feel like a man to beat on a woman?" she yelled at him.

Darkness filled the cabin now. The only light was from a small fire in the fireplace. His evil face was slightly shadowed, giving him an even eerier look.

He backhanded her.

"Your punishment has just begun, Alana."

He pulled out a knife and began to wipe it back and forth on his thigh. He was dressed in camouflage, and he wore a dark green T-shirt that showed off his muscles and his scars. He held her gaze, and she saw how wild and animalistic he looked. He wasn't sane. She understood that. But trying to talk to him was her only option. She couldn't physically fight a Marine, a madman. She needed to be smart and buy herself time.

Neil stared at her. She could feel the evil, the power of his emotions. Her breath caught in her throat, and her body ached everywhere, including her face and her lips.

She didn't know why she said it. Her thoughts were scattered, and she was overwhelmed with fear. But instincts had a strange way of making decisions for people.

"I'm sorry, Neil." She bowed her head and even that brought pain to her shoulders, her neck, and belly.

There was nothing. No response, either verbally or physically, until a few moments later when her heart was racing and she was begging God, someone, to give her the tools, the knowledge to get free from this nightmare

She heard the chair scrape across the dirty wood floor. It fell over and crashed down, but she remained staring down, her hands on her lap over her thighs where she knelt before him.

His military-issued boots came into view, the camouflage green-and-black pants, along with a stance that said he was looking down at her with hatred and disgust.

He gripped her hair and tilted her head back. She gasped and started to react, moving her hands but pulling them back. She kept them on her thighs.

"Please don't hit me again. I can't take it," she said through swollen lips.

"Say it again," he told her in a deep, raspy voice.

To the side, by the window, she saw something. A flash of black, maybe a tiny red light like that on a sniper rifle. Could help be out there? He gave her head a shake, and she cried out.

"I'm sorry. I'm so, so, sorry, Neil."

He pulled her up to her knees. The wood scraped her skin, and she felt it tear her flesh.

He held that grip with one hand and used his other to caress her cheek then move over her neck to her shoulder.

"You're going to have to do better than that, Alana."

She saw the knife on his hip. It was clipped to his waist by a small leather snap. She wondered if she was fast enough to grab it and use it against him.

He pulled her closer.

"I said you'll have to do better than a verbal apology."

He pressed his crotch closer to her, and she understood what he wanted. He wanted her to touch him. To perhaps pleasure him. Could she do it and strike when he was lost in the sensations she gave him? She shivered and nearly gagged just thinking about doing such a thing.

She ran her hands, though still tied together but with about ten inches leeway, up his thighs. Her thumbs hit his crotch, and his cock instantly hardened.

"That's it. Keep going. We've got forever, Alana."

He gave her orders and told her to undo his pants, and she felt the tears roll down her cheeks. She had no control over it, and her mind began to panic and plan.

I'm not going to do this. I won't let him rape me. I won't do what he says. I have to grab the knife. I have to try. I can't do what he's asking of me.

Alana's heart was racing so fast she could hardly swallow or catch her breath. She shook profusely as she reached for his belt and began to undo it. Then she heard the noise. So did Neil, as he turned to see, and she lunged for the knife.

* * * *

Alana's screams could be heard through the cabin walls. Gabe and his team were right behind SWAT as they began to infiltrate the house.

They heard what was happening over the radio. The SWAT commander had a visual and was waiting to make his move. But then someone stepped on a broken plank of wood on the porch, and they had to move in.

They hurried toward the front as canisters of tear gas and explosions of light filled the small cabin.

Then Alana screamed, "No!"

* * * *

She gripped the knife and struck him in the shoulder. The glass shattered, and the room erupted into smoke, and light blinded her. She was hysterical as Neil struck her, and she couldn't see where he was. She caught hold of his head and neck, wrapped her arms around his neck, twisted the rope, and began to pull with all her might, choking him. His back was over her front, crushing her. She had her legs wrapped around his waist, and he kept pounding backward against the ground. Her spine and the backs of her legs ached, and she lost her breath and thought her lungs would collapse. Then there was yelling, and she saw the men in black covered in SWAT gear. She released her hold, and when Neil turned to grab her neck, a shot rang out, the bullet hitting him in the head.

Neil fell to the ground, and she scooted backward, fell onto her back, and cried out in pain.

"Alana, you're okay. It's over, honey. It's over," Gunner told her as he knelt over her and stared at her.

"I need a medic right away. Call the chopper," he said.

"Alana! Alana!"

She could barely keep her eyes open as exhaustion struck her, but she saw Jaxon, Gabe, Geno, Jeb, and Gator before everything went black and she passed out.

Chapter 10

None of them wanted to think about what could have happened to her. As Gunner explained to Gabe, Jaxon, Gator, Geno, and Jeb what was found at Neil's house, they were even more shocked. Neil had definitely lost his mind after leaving the service five years ago. But it was crazy how they came to the conclusion that Neil became obsessed with Alana. Neil had pictures of her throughout his house. He had photographs of her at the clothing boutique, at Casper's, and even at the estate sale. To think that he was the one hiding in that woods watching her over two months was insane.

Gabe looked at Jaxon, who felt responsible.

"I should have been more diligent in protecting her and watching over her. We knew that someone was in the woods. We let the local deputy look into it, but we should have taken care of that ourselves," Jaxon stated through clenched teeth.

They were outside of the hospital room. Alana was resting. She was badly bruised all over and had swelling on her eyes and her cheeks and lips. She had a few bruised ribs and what they thought was internal bleeding that the doctors finally got under control.

"It's not anyone's fault. Who would ever think someone like this would show up in Salvation or Tranquility? She was just being herself. A friendly, outgoing person helping a customer in the store. The guy she helped find a shirt turned out to be a psycho," Gator added.

"I can't let anything like this happen to her, to us, again," Jaxon said.

"We can't let anything like this happen again. We need to make some changes," Geno told them.

"Yes, changes she is going to fight us tooth and nail on," Jeb said.

"She's a daughter of a Marine. I think she'll handle it fine. She did take the knife from Neil, stab him, then put him in a chokehold." Jaxon shook his head then ran his hands through his hair.

"Let's go be with her so she's not alone when she wakes up." Gabe said and turned toward the door.

"Alone? Are you kidding me? This place has been hopping since she got here three days ago. I just want to get her home," Jaxon said.

"So do we, brother. So do we," Gator stated as he placed his hand on Jaxon's shoulder, and they all entered the room.

* * * *

Alana awoke and could hardly open her eyes, but at least she was out of the hospital and with her men. It was the same thing every day, every time she fell asleep and then woke up. Pain. She was starting to get used to it and being bitchy about it too. The guys would curse under their breaths, angry at her injuries and her appearance. She knew she must look pretty bad since everyone was keeping her as far away from mirrors as possible. But with her eyes so swollen and the special cream on them, everything was blurry anyway. At least there wasn't permanent damage or vision damage from what the doctors could tell.

"Hey, sleepy head." She heard Gator's voice, and she moaned softly.

"Easy, baby, don't move. There's no place to get to. Just rest."

"I've been resting forever," she snapped at him.

She felt another hand touch her thigh, and she jerked, scared by the unexpected touch. Alana then cringed, and Gabe cursed.

"Fuck, I'm sorry. I forgot," he told her.

She tried to look at him and felt the tears, and the emotions hit her.

"Don't cry, baby. It will only make the pain worse," Gator said.

"I can't take this. Please help me get up. I have to get out of bed. Help me."

"You had a bath last night. We weren't even supposed to do that. I don't think trekking around in the cool temperatures is a smart idea," Gabe told her.

"I don't care. I'm going insane. Help me."

It took some time and convincing, but finally Gabe and Gator helped her out of bed. They helped her brush her teeth as best they could and then get dressed. Gator lifted her up and carried her downstairs where Jaxon, Geno, and Jeb were preparing lunch.

"We almost have it ready. Did Alana wake up yet?" Jaxon asked as he was fixing the tray of food.

"Yes she did," Alana said, and all three of them turned to look at her.

"What the fuck is she doing out of bed?" Jaxon yelled.

"Jesus. Gator, Gabe she's not supposed to be moving around," Jeb added, running over to her as Gator placed her down onto the chair. She cringed and moaned.

"See?" Geno yelled, raising his hand in the air.

"Just get a cushion or two from the sofa, and I'll be fine," she said.

Jaxon turned away from her and faced the counter. He ran his hand over his face, and she knew he was still so upset at the sight of her injuries.

"We made some chicken soup and grilled cheese. Do you think you can handle that?" Geno asked her as he took the seat next to her and placed his fingers under her chin. She forced a small smile, despite the pain.

"Of course I can. I'm starving," she told him.

He smiled. "That's a good thing."

"Yes, a very good thing," Jeb said and leaned down and kissed her cheek where she wasn't bruised.

Geno walked toward the counter and carried a tray they had prepared to bring her in bed, as they had been doing every day for the past two weeks.

The others poured bowls of soup from the large pot and also plated some grilled cheese sandwiches Jaxon and Geno had made. They all gathered around her at the table, and Jaxon waited to join them.

"Jaxon?"

When she said his name, he stiffened, still looking away from her. She squinted and gulped.

"I can't really see you too well. Are you hiding from me?" she asked. The others stared at their bowls of food and seemed to be pretending to eat.

"Not hiding from you, baby. Just wiping down the stove."

"Well, come join us. I've missed not eating at the table with you guys."

He walked over and sat down with his bowl of soup, way across at the other side.

"Well, that's because you shouldn't be down here yet."

She took a sip from her spoon and let the hot liquid ease down her throat. It actually felt good.

"Says who?" she challenged.

Jaxon put his spoon down.

"Says me, and I'm the one in charge of this family and responsible for everyone's well-being. So eat up, and then it's back to bed."

She lifted the spoon to her mouth and held his gaze as best she could.

"Make me," she said.

Gator chuckled, and then everyone at the table erupted in laughter. She stared at Jaxon, and Jaxon stood up and slammed his fist down on the table.

"I failed you once. I don't intend on failing you again."

Alana placed her spoon down and sat there, staring at him. Everyone at the table went silent.

"Come here, Jaxon," she whispered.

He lowered his head and shook it, and she wondered if he would deny her.

"Am I so ugly now that you no longer want to be close to me?"

"What? No, Alana. No." He stood up and walked over to her.

He knelt down on one knee and placed a hand on the back of her chair then looked down at her hand.

She placed her fingers under his chin and tilted his face toward her.

"You did not fail me. Just as Gabe did not fail me, and neither did his parents or the friends and family in Scrantonville. You did everything you could to find me and rescue me. We're a family. I love you, but I need you, Jaxon. I need all of you, and not to feel sorry for me and avoid looking at me, but to love me, even all banged up and looking like some hideous beast."

"Stop that," Gabe told her.

She glanced at him with a pissed off attitude then looked back at Jaxon.

"Can you love me, Jaxon? Can you stay with me and not look away because you think you failed me and this family?"

He reached up and gently ran his thumb and pointer over her chin where she wasn't bruised.

"I can, doll. I'm sorry for hurting your feelings."

"That's okay. Once I'm feeling better, it will be you who gets the spanking."

The others chuckled.

"I'd like to see you try," he challenged.

"You won't even see it coming," she said, and he leaned forward and gave her a gentle kiss against her swollen lips.

"Now eat up. We need to get you back in tiptop shape. There's only so long I can go without making love to my woman. And I'm getting older. Starting a family needs to start now." He stood up, looking all cocky and in charge.

Alana reached out and slapped his ass.

"Gotcha!" she said, and the men started roaring as laughter filled the air and they teased Jaxon relentlessly.

Alana smiled softly, and her heart lifted with joy and contentedness, for she was in love with her five American soldiers, her Marines, her lovers, her family for life.

THE END

ABOUT THE AUTHOR

People seem to be more interested in my name than where I get my ideas for my stories from. So I might as well share the story behind my name with all my readers.

My momma was born and raised in New Orleans. At the age of twenty, she met and fell in love with an Irishman named Patrick Riley Dwyer. Needless to say, the family was a bit taken aback by this as they hoped she would marry a family friend. It was a modern day arranged marriage kind of thing and my momma downright refused.

Being that my momma's families were descendants of the original English speaking Southerners, they wanted the family blood line to stay pure. They were wealthy and my father's family was poor.

Despite attempts by my grandpapa to make Patrick leave and destroy the love between them, my parents married. They recently celebrated their sixtieth wedding anniversary.

I am one of six children born to Patrick and Lynn Dwyer. I am a combination of both Irish and a true Southern belle. With a name like Dixie Lynn Dwyer it's no wonder why people are curious about my name.

Just as my parents had a love story of their own, I grew up intrigued by the lifestyles of others. My imagination as well as my need to stray from the straight and narrow made me into the woman I am today.

Enjoy *The American Soldier Collection 11: Mending Hearts* and allow your imagination to soar freely.

For all titles by Dixie Lynn Dwyer, please visit
www.bookstrand.com/dixie-lynn-dwyer

Siren Publishing, Inc.
www.SirenPublishing.com

Lightning Source UK Ltd.
Milton Keynes UK
UKOW06f1920040615

252923UK00014B/251/P